LET ME HOLD YOU

Books by Jan Thompson

Protector Sweethearts (6 Books)
JanThompson.com/protector

Defender Sweethearts (6 Books)
JanThompson.com/defender

Binary Hackers (4 Books)
JanThompson.com/binary

Seaside Chapel (7 Books)
JanThompson.com/seaside

Savannah Sweethearts (12 Books)
JanThompson.com/savannah

Vacation Sweethearts (8 Books)
JanThompson.com/vacation

Midtown Christmas (4 Books)
JanThompson.com/christmas

LET ME HOLD YOU

Big City Romance, Small Town Feel

Midtown Christmas
Book 1

JAN THOMPSON

GEORGIA
PRESS

Let Me Hold You (Midtown Christmas Book 1)

To my Lord and Savior, Jesus Christ, who died on the cross to save me from my sins and rose again from the grave to give me eternal life in heaven.

For God so loved the world that He gave His only begotten Son, that whoever believes in Him should not perish but have everlasting life.
—John 3:16

Read a FREE eBook in the Same Story World

Set in Georgia, South Carolina, and Tennessee, this clean and wholesome Christian romance tells the story of art gallery archivist Sheryl Breckenridge and world-famous sculptor Winton Pace. Read this ebook for free!

Time for Me (A Vacation Sweethearts Prequel)
JanThompson.com/time-free

About Let Me Hold You

MIDTOWN CHRISTMAS BOOK 1

She wants to get out of his friend zone and into his heart.

After breaking up with his girlfriend, Levi meets the woman of his dreams, but she rejects him in his tale of unrequited love. His best friend,

Maggie, tries to help him to pursue his dream date without revealing that she's secretly in love with him. Will these two friends find a breakthrough and their own happily ever?

Lonesome Levi

After breaking up with his girlfriend, church warehouse manager Levi Theroux finds comfort in his best friend, Maggie. However, his heart can't imagine her as more than his best friend, and he looks elsewhere for a new girlfriend, someone who can fill in the space left behind by his ex.

While working at the Midtown Village ministry arm of Midtown Chapel, Levi falls for someone—but she rejects him, unfortunately. As she happens to be a friend of Maggie's, Levi wants her to be his matchmaker and get him that dream girl. Will Maggie take the job? She has to. She's the only one among his friends whom he trusts fully.

Matchmaker Maggie

Women's ministry administrative assistant Maggie Jacobs has fallen in love with Levi after his breakup, and looks forward to seeing him every day as they minister at the Midtown Village of tiny homes for needy families, single parents, and emancipated homeless teens. From November to January, this place turns into a Christmas Village with little shops and lots of seasonal activities.

However, she won't tell him about her feelings because he has not shown any romantic interest in her. Maybe she isn't his type or something. Now he wants her to help him pursue the chef in the church kitchen. How many ways can he break her heart without even realizing it? Still, she can't say no to him. Perhaps she has to accept the fact that they would only ever be friends. Or does she? Either way, Maggie sees a dead-end to any romantic relationship. To protect her heart, Maggie decides to leave town...

A big-city romance with a small-town feel set in midtown Atlanta, Georgia, *Let Me Hold You* is Book 1 in *USA Today* bestselling author Jan Thompson's **Midtown Christmas** holiday series. Maggie and Levi's romance is a spin-off of *Pray for Me* (Vacation Sweethearts Book 5). Levi is cousin to Cyrus Theroux, the co-owner of the Christmastown holiday decorating company in *Wish You Joy* (Savannah Sweethearts Book 10).

Unrequited love. Secret love. Best friends. Friend zone. Friends to more. Slow burn. Midtown Atlanta. Big city romance. Church life. Women in Ministry.

If you like this Christmas story, you might also like the other books in this collection.

- Book 1: *Let Me Hold You*
- Book 2: *Let Me Adore You*
- Book 3: *Let Me Honor You*
- Book 4: *Let Me Love You*

Sign up for Jan's newsletter to be notified when the next novels in this series are published: JanThompson.com/newsletter

LET ME HOLD YOU

Chapter One

"Three! Two! One!" the crowd shouted in unison.

Standing by the Christmas tree in the center of the Midtown Village tiny-house community square, Pastor Eldon Kim pressed the big button on his hand-held remote. The lights on the twenty-foot tree sparkled in the cold November evening, the night after Thanksgiving Day.

On cue, residents flicked on their porch lights, and all their outdoor decorations came alive, brightly lighting up the rows of tiny houses around the square. The lights turned Midtown Village into its seasonal name of Christmas Village.

Cheers went up...but one heart sank to the ground.

Maggie Jacobs clapped as loudly as everyone

else, her hands cold, and her smile masking the sadness and loneliness within. She zipped up her long goose-down coat and dug her hands into the insulated pockets.

Not alone per se, because she knew that God was with her, and her church friends were all around her.

But loneliness was a different thing.

A painful feeling of emotional isolation gripped her heart and there was no panacea. All she could do was leave this place and never return. Her brother waited for her in Florida, and perhaps in his small community of Lakeside, she'd make new friends and find a partner in life.

But all was lost in Atlanta.

She looked around the Village and knew that the festivities would end in the first week of January when the two city blocks returned to their real name of Midtown Village. That would be one week after Maggie had packed up her worldly belongings and driven away.

Goodbye.

"Bittersweet" was the word she'd been experiencing all evening.

This was Maggie's last Christmas in Midtown Village, at Midtown Chapel, and for that matter, in midtown Atlanta. She'd been there since Midtown

Village used to be called Midtown Chapel Village, back in the early days of trial and error, when the first tiny home was constructed. Maggie had been in college then, excited about a new opportunity to minister to needy families by providing for them a roof over their heads and three meals a day.

In the distance, a siren blared, jarring her from her memories, reminding her of the big city she had lived in her whole life. Seven years ago, she'd stayed in town after earning her bachelor's degree in communications, when Midtown Chapel hired her right away to be the ministry assistant to the pastor's wife, Lydia Kim, who was the women's ministry director at that time.

When Mrs. Kim had taken a break to care for her ailing mother, the church hired Tally Fitz-patrick—now Tally Moss—who kept Maggie in the same position.

In fact, Maggie and Tally had become friends in those five years they had worked together. If Maggie were to ever marry, she'd ask Tally to be her matron of honor.

Maggie sighed. She might be single for many years to come, if not her entire life.

After Tally had married and moved to the Bahamas, the position of women's ministry director went back to the pastor's wife. Mrs. Kim took the director position with the understanding that she would not manage Midtown Village.

The church spun off the tiny-house community into a nonprofit organization with new management. It even had a board of directors that was comprised of Midtown pastors and donors.

Since then, the new Village manager, Bina Marley, had gone through numerous administrative assistants. After firing the last one, she had taken months to find a new assistant she could work with. Every time Bina let someone go, Maggie had to do the work.

Maggie thanked God when the church finally hired Erika Song to fill in the administrative assistant position. Bina assigned her training to Maggie.

Once she finished training Erika, Maggie would only have one job left as the women's ministry administrative assistant—half the workload she had been used to under Tally.

Maggie had been adjusting to the new changes. The work arrangement was not the same as when Tally had been the women's ministry director.

Regardless of the changes in leadership, Maggie still loved working there. Truth be told, she didn't want to move away from Midtown Chapel, her home church for life.

Still, that wasn't why Maggie was leaving town.

She had to, though. She could no longer stay in Atlanta.

And the reason was ambling toward her, two mugs in his hands, cutting through the crowd with a smile on his face, under the street lamps and racing Christmas tree lights.

Levi Theroux, sporting a new beard he'd been trying to grow for months, handed her a mug. "Hot cocoa. No sugar. A couple of drops of honey. Just the way you like it."

"You know me well."

"How can I not? You're my best friend."

Best friend forever.

Precisely the reason Maggie couldn't stay.

Levi looked around furtively—Maggie had to laugh—and then he lowered his voice. "I saw Forsythia in the kitchen when I was making your cocoa. She won't talk to me. Have you spoken to her about you-know-what?"

Ah, the date.

It had been all Levi could talk about the last few months whenever he saw Maggie. Forsythia this and Forsythia that. It drove Maggie up the wall.

The woman wasn't interested in Levi, okay? What more could Maggie do? Just because she had known Forsythia for a whole year didn't mean she could persuade the chef to go out with Levi—especially after his botched attempt to befriend her at the last singles outing.

The only way Maggie could think of to make Levi happy—and get him off her back—would be to somehow get Forsythia to have dinner with him.

It would take a miracle.

Forsythia was interested in someone else. She always was. Unfortunately, nobody on her list was named Levi.

"Why are you doing this to me?" Maggie muttered.

"What? Did you say something about Forsythia?"

At this point, Maggie wanted to slap herself, but didn't get a chance to do that because someone tapped her shoulder. She turned around to find the pastor's wife standing there.

"Mrs. Kim, how are you this evening?" Maggie asked.

"Fine, thank you. Are you staying warm in this cold weather?" Mrs. Kim's voice was gentle and kind, the type of voice that one would want to hear in a crisis.

And Maggie wanted to tell Mrs. Kim everything about her problems with Levi, but she couldn't.

Maybe *wouldn't* was a better word.

It was too embarrassing to talk about.

So Maggie's only recourse was to run away. Leave this place and go home to her brother. Florida was far enough away, wasn't it?

"Yes, this hot cocoa that Levi made warms me up." Maggie lifted the mug in the air.

"If you like, I can make you a cup of cocoa too," Levi said to Mrs. Kim.

"No, thanks. But I need to borrow Maggie for a few minutes, if I may."

"Sure. I have to go anyway. Got some errands to run. Then turning in early tonight. I'll be back tomorrow morning—here—and then I have to go to the warehouse all afternoon."

"Lots of donations?"

"Yes, ma'am. A children's clothing outlet closed down and donated all their brand-new clothes to us. New lumber came in yesterday, taking up space. Tomorrow morning, we're getting five tiny-home kits, and I don't know where to put them all. We're running out of space if we don't get rid of something or other."

"Do you want some help organizing your inventory?" Mrs. Kim patted Maggie's shoulder. "Here we have the most amazing organizer I know. I think you will have room for everything if she gives you a hand."

Maggie didn't say anything. She did not want to "go over there and help" Levi. No, she did not want to see him at all.

Besides, the warehouse was Levi's area. Why had Mrs. Kim suggested that Maggie interfere?

"In the spirit of helping one another, we're going to do something interesting next year at church," Mrs. Kim said. "Well, a few interesting things, but one of them will be cross training. We'll do a work week in which we'll challenge all the ministries to allow other ministry workers to work in their areas all week. That should answer the question of whether one person's job is harder than other people's, you know?"

Mrs. Kim was so unlike Maggie's previous boss. While Tally worked within the system and scope of the women's ministry, Mrs. Kim often made suggestions that affected and benefited the entire church. Obviously, she had better access to the pastor since they had been married for decades, but Mrs. Kim was also well-respected by the deacons, who listened to her suggestions every time she came up with them—at least one a month.

"Maybe you can be my test case, and go over to the warehouse and work on their inventory database for a day there, and send me a report," Mrs. Kim said to Maggie, who had spent time at the warehouse as a part of her job as a ministry assistant, but not in any other capacity.

Suddenly, all the things Maggie had to do in December tumbled through her mind like clothes in a dryer on high heat. One more thing wouldn't hurt, but why did it have to be in the warehouse where Levi worked?

Maggie felt annoyed. Christmas was all around her and she should be enjoying the pretty lights lining the tiny homes and community center. But no, Levi had made her upset and she felt like crying.

"However, I can't spare her all next week as we're wrapping up training for Erika," Mrs. Kim said to Levi.

"No problem. I'll wait."

"The only time Maggie can go help you is a Saturday—either tomorrow or next Saturday." Mrs. Kim turned to Maggie. "Don't forget to take the day off during the week when you work on Saturdays."

Maggie nodded. "Tomorrow won't work out though. I have to be here all day so I can't go to the warehouse."

Maggie knew why Levi hadn't gotten this over-abundance of inventory rehoused sooner. Like way before this busy Christmas time.

It had been a year and nine months since he'd

broken up with Soline. The first year had been bad for Levi as he reeled from his loss. There was no way he could've competed with his ex-girlfriend's first love.

His feeling of despair had driven Levi to Maggie and her older brother, Malachi, an ordained pastor. They had comforted Levi and ministered to him. Eventually, Malachi had to leave Atlanta to become the assistant pastor of Lakeside Chapel in Florida.

Levi had continued to hang out with Maggie. He seemed to be on the mend until he spotted Forsythia. He snapped out of his doldrums and fixed his attention on the Midtown Chapel kitchen chef de cuisine. She was all he could think of now.

Little did he know that *he* had been all Maggie could think of in the last several months—well, besides God and her ministry at church.

"I thought we distributed all the Christmas decorations for the homes," Levi said.

Maggie nodded. "I'll be helping to decorate the community center."

"You do too much."

Maggie ignored Levi's words. "I want to do it."

She didn't say that being among people in the Village dispelled her loneliness. Her house felt empty now that her brother had moved to Lakeside. She liked hanging out with Levi, but he would move on as soon as he found himself a girlfriend.

"Then I'll help too." Levi made a commitment.

"You're the best." Mrs. Kim gave him two thumbs up.

"How about helping me organize the warehouse next Saturday?" Levi looked at Maggie.

"Hold this." She handed her mug of cocoa to Levi. Then she retrieved her phone from her crossbody purse and checked her calendar for next week. It was packed.

"The singles Christmas party is that evening, and I have to bake all day." She put away her phone and took the mug back from Levi.

Levi looked at her kinda funny. "You don't bake."

"I've learned a few things."

"You googled."

"So?"

"What are you baking?"

"I thought I'd make some gingerbread cookies." Why not? She could try new things, right? She got tired of having to always buy store-bought products whenever the singles at church had a gathering. A number of the other single women cooked. Forsythia, for example. And Levi loved home cooking.

Oh, what am I thinking?

Maggie reminded herself not to compete with Chef Forsythia McDevitt, who had worked for years at Piper's Place in Savannah, Georgia, and who had appeared in numerous chef magazines.

That Forsythia.

Someone Maggie shouldn't try to compete with.

"You've never made gingerbread cookies—or any cookies—in your life without burning them or forgetting an ingredient of some sort," Levi reminded her.

Rub it in, will you?

Maggie's shoulders sagged. "You're right. I better not try at all."

Levi shook his head. "No, no. You must try. Tell you what. I'll come over and we can bake together. Then we can carpool to the Christmas dinner and save gas money."

Another reason Maggie had to leave Atlanta, leave Georgia, leave, leave, leave…

If she didn't, Levi would walk into her activities all the time. She couldn't get rid of him even if she tried. Sure, she wanted him to spend many happy moments with her, but there was a barrier between them that she couldn't break through.

"What a nice friend you have." Mrs. Kim didn't show one way or another whether she knew anything about Maggie's relationship with Levi.

Friend.

Exactly. That was all she would ever be to Levi.

Often, he'd call her his "best friend," but they could never go beyond platonic.

As a friend, Levi often came to the women's ministry office to lounge on the couch and chat with Maggie whenever he wasn't helping her to move this or that for the Midtown Village or the church warehouse. He was very good at moving things.

He even moved Maggie's heart.

Yeah, right into "park" in the friend zone.

Chapter Two

S ingle and free.

Sure. He'd been single and free for at least one year and nine months since he'd broken up with Soline and watched her first love propose to her at Tally's wedding.

Single? Yes.

Free? No.

Not at all.

He felt that something was missing from his life—the companion he believed God would give him so he wouldn't be alone in his thirties.

He had tried to explain that to Soline, but she had warned him not to put her on a pedestal. That was two days before she dumped him and returned to her first love.

Good for her.

Levi wished them well.

As far as he knew, the marriage had taken place, so he wasn't about to get Soline back.

He had let her go.

Maggie had told him that he must.

Maggie.

The only person who understood what he had felt these months, who sat there and listened to him without judging him or calling him out on anything—even though he knew he'd been wrong to cling to Soline so much that she suffocated.

Maggie Jacobs.

"Truly, she's my best friend." He hoped he hadn't mumbled too loudly, but he was the only person in his vintage red Ford pickup truck.

He didn't know how long he'd been sitting there in the parking lot of the Midtown Village—oh, Christmas Village—but it was only six o'clock in the morning and he was having coffee.

He'd forgotten to stop at a drive-through to pick up breakfast, but he knew there'd be food in the community center. Chef Forsythia and her crew should be there soon, if they weren't already there. Lunch was free for all volunteers.

For Levi, this was yet another day of work. He had opted not to take a day off during the week even if he worked on Saturdays because he'd rather use the eight bonus hours for time off here and there. Maybe he could leave work an hour or two early on a weekday to buy a gift for Forsythia or something.

Wait. What?

He knew he was getting ahead of himself.

A rap on the window startled him.

Maggie stood there, with a lifted hand holding a paper sack of some sort. She was wearing her usual zipped-up chocolate-colored coat. As far as Levi knew, the goose-down coat was a gift from her older brother.

She looked nice and warm against the dawn and sidewalk lights all around the parking lot.

Levi rolled down his window. He could hear distant city traffic and a few sirens. "Good morning, love."

"Not your *love*. Stop teasing me." She waved the paper bag. "Chicken, cheese, and bacon on an English muffin. Still hot."

Levi reached out to get it. The bag was hot. "Have you eaten?"

"No. Just arrived."

"Aren't we both early risers." Levi patted the passenger seat. "Eat with me."

"Okay." Maggie walked around the truck and climbed into the passenger side.

"What have you got?" Levi sprayed hand sanitizer on Maggie's palms and then on his own.

"Same."

"We are like two peas in a pod." Levi rolled up his window. "We like the same breakfast."

"Sometimes I have pancakes."

"Me too." Levi said grace and they dug into their chicken breakfast.

After a while, Levi looked away.

Maggie said not a single word. She chewed her food quietly.

That was one of the things Levi liked about her. She could have said, "What's wrong?"

But she didn't.

She simply sat there and ate silently.

Sometimes Levi didn't know what went through Maggie's mind, but she probably knew all about him because he'd been talking nonstop for a year and nine months, pouring out his heart like a crybaby.

If God allowed Soline to marry someone else, then she's not for you, is she?

Maggie had said those words only once to Levi, but he hadn't forgotten.

"I've let Soline go like a million times." Levi put his hand down on his thigh. The jeans were not insulated, and his goose-down jacket only went down to his hip. The heater in the car made up for the deficit.

Maggie nodded. She continued eating.

"I think if I date someone else, it proves that I've moved on."

Maggie was silent.

"Are you praying?" Levi asked.

Maggie looked up. "I was thinking."

"About what?"

"About you."

"Does that mean you've figured out a way for Forsythia to agree to go to dinner with me?" Levi raised his eyebrows.

"I wasn't thinking about that." Maggie's voice was even-keeled. That was one of her strengths, really, and why she was such a good ministry assistant. No matter how many complaints she received from people on the waiting list for the next tiny home, she remained calm and collected and cool.

Levi decided not to ask what Maggie was thinking about. He had more important matters to deal with. "Have you talked to Forsythia about me?"

"It would be awkward, you know?" Maggie took a last bite. She crumpled the brown paper liner and threw it into her paper sack.

"She knows I'm interested in her. Maybe you can prod her."

"Prod? Like for cattle? That's cruel."

"I meant a nudge. Just a little push."

"You might end up pushing her away," Maggie warned.

Levi sank back into his driver's seat.

They sat in silence until Levi had finished his breakfast.

Maggie glanced at her watch. "I have to run."

"Thank you for the breakfast. Next time it's my turn."

"Okay." Maggie was about to open the door when Levi reached for her coat sleeve and stopped her.

"Look at me," he said.

Maggie did. "What?"

Levi used the napkin in his hand to wipe a couple of crumbs off the edge of Maggie's lips. They were pink and soft—the lips, not the crumbs.

Maggie frowned. "Is that napkin clean?"

"Slightly used. But it's my saliva if anything."

"Ewwwww! Go away!" She scrambled out of the truck, slammed the door, and sprinted down the sidewalk.

Levi laughed. He could have used a new tissue paper from the box, or he could've told Maggie to wipe her own lips.

But he'd done what he'd done.

Why?

He had no idea.

He checked the dashboard clock. It said 5:34 a.m., which meant it was 6:34 a.m. He should get the clock fixed soon, but not today. Right now, he was busy trying to get a date with Forsythia.

Forsythia was only two years younger than he was, compared to Maggie's four. Forsythia always carried herself like a lady, even in the kitchen at church. He had heard her belting out orders on Wednesday nights during the church supper in the fellowship hall. Even her loud voice sounded sweet to Levi.

"Am I in love?" Levi asked aloud.

He knew exactly where Forsythia would be this morning, and he had decided to go to the kitchen to volunteer. After all, there was nothing much else he could do since he had done his duty as the warehouse manager.

The system that Tally Moss, née Fitzpatrick, had set in place for years had worked, and Levi saw no reason to fix it.

First, back in October, everyone who lived in a tiny home at the Midtown Village would log in online into the request database. They would browse the warehouse catalog to see what decorations they wanted for their front porch and interior.

One week ago, Levi had distributed all the requested decorations in labeled boxes. Then he flew to Savannah for Thanksgiving with his cousin, Cyrus, his wife, Amy, and their three kids.

By the time he returned to work on the Friday after Thanksgiving, he'd had nothing to do but help set up the twenty-foot Christmas tree in the Village square.

Today, he had cleared his schedule to go help as close to the kitchen as possible so that he could be in view of Forsythia. Perhaps if she saw him enough, she'd agreed to go out with him—even though she'd already turned him down twice.

Today, his secret weapon was Maggie, whom he'd recruited as his matchmaker.

"Maggie, you're the best," he remembered telling her. She must have been super moved, because she'd had tears in her eyes.

Levi had no idea his words meant so much to Maggie. He made a note to himself to compliment her more.

He locked his pickup truck and carried his brown bag to the nearest trash can. He waved to a few people hanging more lights on their tiny porches.

Most of the tiny-home residents had set up shops on their front porches where they'd sell arts and crafts, or canned fruits and vegetables. He spotted jars of peaches and remembered Aunt Marie. When she had been alive, she'd enjoyed peaches and couldn't get enough of them.

Maybe a jar of peaches could be his Christmas present for Maggie as well. She liked peaches too, although she didn't like the syrup. Too sweet for her. She'd never had a sweet tooth. No wonder she was in good shape even without exercising daily or going to the gym at all.

As Levi walked closer to the community center, he saw active church member Alden Benson chatting with Maggie at the front door.

Alden was smiling from ear to ear. Tall and beta male—with flawless skin—he made Levi want to throw up.

Stay away from Maggie, you!

The words lodged in his throat, as it had always been. Oh, if only Levi were braver and more competitive. He'd sprint up there and walk into the building with Maggie.

But he didn't.

He stood there, watching the interaction from far away.

Maggie was smiling shyly.

What? Why was she shy? Maggie had never been shy around Levi. Why would she be shy around Alden?

"I better go protect her from whatever Alden

has in mind." He quickened his steps, but it was too late.

Alden entered the building right behind Maggie—too close, as though they had arrived together—and the glass door closed behind them.

All of Levi wanted to chase after them and stand in between Maggie and Alden, but his phone rang. He almost ignored it until he saw that it was his cousin Cyrus.

He had to take the call.

Cyrus had been waiting for a reply about the Christmastown job prospect for Levi. Granted, Cyrus's warehouse director in Savannah would still need to interview Levi.

"I've promoted Rasheed to regional director. Right now he's planning his schedule for January. He will be in Atlanta scouting for a new warehouse location for our metro Atlanta branch. He said he can interview you at that time."

"Thank you for thinking of me. I'm still praying about it." Levi walked away from the community center to get some privacy on the lawn. He tried not to mention "job offer" so that no one at the Village would misunderstand the phone conversation.

"Rasheed has about five people in mind, and you're on his shortlist because of your experience at the church warehouse—even though the Christmastown warehouse is ten times bigger."

It had been a week since Levi had received the email from his cousin about the Christmastown expansion to inland Georgia and potentially westward to Alabama and northward to Tennessee, North Carolina, and South Carolina. Savannah would still be the holiday decorating company's headquarters, but metropolitan Atlanta was a bigger distribution hub if Christmastown were to expand to the entire southeast instead of just along coastal Georgia.

Cyrus was ambitious about growing their family business, and he wanted Levi involved in it. It wasn't a shoo-in, to be sure, because Levi had to meet with Rasheed Bolton. If Levi failed the interview with Rasheed, his bachelor's degree in business administration and ten years of warehouse management skills would mean nothing.

"Could I let you know after Christmas?" Levi boldly asked, knowing it could be the end of the job prospect.

"One month from now? Sure. We're not interviewing until the second week of January so you have time."

"Great. Thank you."

"You pray about it thoroughly. If you think the Lord is leading you to us—maybe to provide more salary and health insurance to support your future wife and kids—then click on the link I emailed you and submit your résumé."

Future wife and kids?

Right now, Levi was merely trying to get back into dating.

Then again, there were logistics involved. Levi wondered if he should seriously consider getting into Christmastown early—before they found a location to build their new warehouse. Then he could be on the search committee to find the right warehouse site that wouldn't be too far away from his current life. Metro Atlanta was a huge place, and if the warehouse ended up being far away from downtown Atlanta, it could mean a long commute to church for Levi.

He wanted to continue attending Midtown Chapel and have easy access to the church—and to Maggie at the women's ministry office.

Oh, and Forsythia too. Let's not forget the dream date.

On the other hand, even if he was the cousin of the company president, it didn't mean Levi could move the needle in their corporate decisions. If Levi waited until Christmastown confirmed the location of the new warehouse, he could then decide whether he should bother applying for the position as their new warehouse manager.

After all, he loved his job at the Midtown warehouse. It was small, but it served the church ministries. Levi couldn't expect a pay raise because the church relied on donations to run the warehouse, but Levi had less stress working there and therefore could spend more time with Maggie—

Oh, and getting his dream date.

In that split second, Levi began to doubt himself. Did he really want to chase after Forsythia when he made almost all of his decisions with his one and only best friend, Maggie, in mind?

Speaking of whom, his buddy was inside the community center right now with Alden, and he had to go look and see. He turned around and headed toward the community center.

"I'm not hurrying you, Levi," Cyrus said.

"I know."

"I'm also not trying to recruit you even though your skillset matches what we need in next year's expansion to the southeast with Atlanta as a hub."

"Thank you for considering me at all."

"I've known you since you were born, and I know that when you can't decide which way to go, you sometimes come to a standstill at the fork in the road, and you don't move for a long time."

"You know me well, cousin."

"When you pray about this potential, consider the bigger picture that God might have in mind."

"I will pray about the pros and cons."

"If there is no one to take over your job at the church warehouse, then you might choose to stay there," Cyrus said. "If you think you can continue to serve God in our Christian company—even though we do sell secular Christmas decorations in addition to all the religious ones—then give us a shot."

"I get it. Thank you, Cyrus. I appreciate you for taking the pressure off me in this decision." Levi didn't lower his voice when he reached the warehouse entrance. "Regardless of the outcome, may all glory go to God."

"All I want to hear."

"I'll let you go, Cy." *I'm on a rescue mission.*

Levi hung up. As he entered the community center, his eyes scanned left and right for Maggie. Hmm. Maybe she was in the storage room looking for lights and ornaments.

Someone called his name. It was one of his security guards at the warehouse, here this morning to help get the Christmas Village set up. He waved to Levi.

Levi spotted Forsythia in the hallway near the security guard, and Levi made a beeline to his colleague and gym friend standing next to a pushcart.

"Pete called in sick and we need an extra

hand." The guard wore the same Christmas sweater from last year—that his grandmother had knitted for him. "The donation trailer is out back, and Miss Forsythia wanted it emptied today. We are shorthanded and need to move some giant boxes to the kitchen pantry."

"For next week's soup kitchen." Levi had been the one who decided to park the trailer in the Village parking lot instead of at the church warehouse fifteen minutes away.

Another reason to get Maggie to the warehouse to look over the inventory.

Chapter Three

$\mathcal{C}$ompared to Alden—always upbeat and rarely showing what bothered him—Maggie might be too easy to read, often wearing her feelings on her sleeves.

How could she not when Levi was over there at the far end of the community center where the kitchen was, practically following Chef Forsythia around like a puppy.

Maybe that was a bit harsh.

Maggie closed her eyes, drew a deep breath, and tried to pray. No words came. Who would she be praying for? Herself? Levi?

In fewer than four weeks, she would leave Atlanta and none of these things would matter. Levi could date anyone he wanted. She'd try to move on and start over in Florida.

It would be hard for her to let Levi go, since it had been three long years of seeing him daily. On Sundays, they attended the same Sunday school and church service. On Mondays through Fridays, they worked at the same church. And then on Saturdays, sometimes Levi went over to her house to test new breakfast recipes in her kitchen. He said it was easier to cook for two people than for one.

However, she had to let him go for her own sanity.

After all, she could never tell him that she had developed feelings for him. It would be too embarrassing. Besides, Levi treated her like a platonic friend—leaning toward becoming siblings rather than anything else.

She sighed.

A large waving hand appeared in front of her.

Maggie blinked.

"You're facing the wrong direction." Alden put two hands on her shoulders and turned her around to face the wall behind an eight-foot ladder and two big boxes filled with either wreaths or string lights.

Bolted to the wall was a series of four connected panels showing a giant panoramic painting, à la Currier and Ives, spanning from one end of the wall to the other. Three art students from church had painted this trompe l'oeil that showed a winter scene beyond a sidewalk of lampposts.

"Ah yes, the lampposts." They were life-size. And why Maggie and Alden were there today.

"Which end shall we start at?" Alden asked.

"Doesn't matter. I guess we could go left to right. There are five lampposts, and we just need to hang wreaths on the posts. Then we hang lights on the trees."

"Are there nails for the wreaths and lights?" Alden stepped toward one of the panels. "Yes, I see. There are hooks."

"The artists made sure we don't hammer on their painting." Maggie laughed. "They even picked the wreaths for us that are not too heavy."

Alden started moving the ladder. "Why don't they just hang the wreaths and lights themselves?"

"Got to leave us something to do, right? After all, the painting is free for us to display." Maggie pushed the box of wreaths on the floor behind Alden.

When she got the box where she wanted, Levi was standing in front of her, a hot cup of something in his hand. "Want some cocoa?"

Before Maggie could say anything, Alden spoke up. "We barely started and you're taking a break already? This thirty-minute project could take all day."

Maggie took the mug from Levi and handed it to Alden. "For you."

Levi didn't say anything.

"Thank you, Levi." Maggie went back for the second box.

"What's he up to?" Levi whispered loud enough for only Maggie to hear.

"What do you mean?"

Levi carried the box. Maggie walked alongside him.

"He seems awfully close to you these days."

"Really?" Maggie was surprised Levi had noticed. "Does it bother you?"

Levi didn't directly answer her question. "What does he want from you?"

Maggie shrugged. "He's a nice guy."

"Is that all?"

"Church member. Missions committee." Maggie didn't know Alden well enough to know his church activities.

"So? Stay away from him."

Levi's voice sounded like he was frustrated or something.

"How can I?" Maggie chuckled. "He's Hiroki's admin assistant. You know our church has hired Hiroki to develop that piece of kitty-corner lot that Mrs. Arnold left us in her will. The women's ministry and the Midtown Village are working closely with Hiroki on this project. It could be a year before all is done."

Ruttledge Yamada Urquhart Commercial Properties had branched out into residential properties, and Hiroki Yamada was now in charge of the subsidiary. Maggie didn't want to keep talking about them like she was going to be actively involved in the following year.

Yeah, she still hadn't told Levi that she was leaving Midtown Chapel and taking up a new job at Lakeside Resort in Florida. How could she break it to him? She decided to wait until after Christmas.

Make it last-minute and run out the door.

"Why not let Bina and Erika liaise with Hiroki and Alden?"

It wasn't Maggie's place to tell Levi that Village manager Bina Marley had been suffering from migraine headaches the last six months and had to take time off from work. Maggie and Mrs. Kim had been covering for her as Erika was still newly employed.

"As you know, I'll be training Erika this week." Maggie pointed to the floor space where she wanted Levi to put the box of lights.

"Then you'd just be in Mrs. Kim's office?"

"Something like that." Oh, she felt bad about keeping so many secrets from Levi, but sooner or later, she'd have to sit down with him and explain that she was leaving town for good, and there was no way he would be able to change her mind.

In the meantime, what she said to him was technically the truth. She would be in Mrs. Kim's office. But only for four more weeks.

"Thank you for your help, Levi." Maggie looked toward the kitchen and spotted Forsythia. She pointed.

Levi turned to look, but he didn't leave.

Maggie was somewhat surprised that Levi didn't chase after Forsythia. What could she say to Levi in front of Alden without arousing suspicions?

"Aren't you supposed to be helping in the food pantry or somewhere?" Maggie finally asked.

Levi nodded. "I wanted to bring you some hot cocoa. Didn't expect you to give it to him."

Alden sipped up the last drop of cocoa. He handed the mug back to Levi. "Thank you, brother."

Levi took the mug wordlessly.

Maggie waved him away, and began to climb the ladder that Alden had set up by the first lamppost on the wall painting.

"No, no." Alden stopped her. "You hand me the wreaths and hold the ladder."

"Ooh, you're bossy."

Alden smiled. "Do I have a choice? Remember what happened last Christmas?"

Maggie would have forgotten if Alden hadn't brought it up.

"You tripped on a pile of lights on the floor and sprained your ankle." Alden put a foot on the bottom rung of the eight-foot ladder. He motioned to Maggie to hand him a wreath.

Maggie did so. "Apples and oranges, Alden. The hallway was poorly lit. I didn't see the strands on the floor."

"If you were clumsy at ground level, what would happen when you climb up a ladder?" Alden hung the wreath, climbed down the ladder, and moved it to the next lamppost. "This is why I'm here today on my day off. I'll do the hard work and you enjoy the show."

"Show? Are you showing off that your love language is acts of service?" Maggie laughed. They were also in the same Sunday school class, and one time everyone had shared what their love languages were.

For Maggie, she only wanted to hear nice words from one person and spend quality time with him, and she wasn't going to ever get it the way she wanted.

What was Levi's love language? He had been out of town that Sunday morning and missed the roundtable discussion. Even after she asked him, Levi didn't want to take the test to find out what his love language was. However, knowing him long enough, Maggie guessed that it was also acts of service.

Was she attracted to men who had this type of love language? Well, she hadn't even considered Alden, so maybe that was the wrong question.

Alden stepped on the ladder, a wreath hanging off the crook of his elbow.

"I don't think I'll fall off the ladder." Maggie held the ladder, even though it seemed strong enough to hold Alden.

He was six feet tall, maybe a couple of inches shorter than Levi, but Alden was fit and trim. Maggie knew he worked out at the gym every morning before work because he had invited her to come along and get some exercise that she badly needed.

The gym was only two miles from church, so Maggie could have gone. However, she had made the decision to focus her time on Levi.

Well, that had been in the past.

Now she was letting him go.

Slowly.

Really, she could turn her attention on Alden, and he wouldn't mind. In fact, he had sent her signals that he wanted to be more than colleagues at work. She recalled the times he'd been extra attentive to her at Village meetings. Later, he'd told her that he had volunteered to be a part of the Christmas Village planning committee because of her.

When Maggie hadn't responded, Alden hadn't pushed her. That was how he was. She had known him for a year, and he'd never once been unkind to her. Always helpful, always going out of his way to make life at work easier for her. Best colleague ever, if there ever was a reward for that.

Since the church had acquired the new lot next door, Maggie found herself working more with Alden. Both of them were administrative assistants and they talked to each other more than to their bosses.

Maggie wondered if she should move on from Levi. Her secret love for him couldn't last. It was eating her up and stressing her out every time he went on a date or pursued his unrequited love because he'd tell her about it and ask her for advice and so forth.

Of course she had to help him. If not for their

friendship, there was nothing left for Maggie to hang onto.

At this point, Maggie didn't see a path forward for her and Levi. Levi only considered her his friend. Best friends or not, they would still only be friends.

Perhaps Alden was there because this was their story. Maggie felt like a second female lead in some romantic drama.

She chuckled.

"A Christmas cookie for your thought," Alden said from the top of the ladder.

"Huh?" Maggie's eyes were elsewhere. The kitchen door in the distance opened, and Forsythia pushed a cart. Next to her, Levi was carrying a box and talking a mile a minute. Forsythia said not a word.

"What was that chuckle about? The curious want to know." Alden droned on.

When Maggie didn't answer, he continued. "Do I look that bad from this angle?"

Maggie sighed. "Focus, Alden. Don't fall off the ladder."

He climbed down. Smiled at her. "Ah, you care."

"Liability. Technically you're only a volunteer today. You don't work at Midtown Chapel. I do.

The Christmas Village doesn't need broken-bone publicity."

"I'll be careful." He moved the ladder.

Maggie followed him with another wreath. "Hey, how long have you known Forsythia?"

"Longer than I've known you." Alden hung the wreath. "She used to work at Piper's Place on River Street in Savannah."

"I know. I've been there. Riverside Church is sister church to Midtown, and their church members eat at that restaurant often."

"I ate there a lot too when I worked at our Savannah office. Piper's Place still caters RYUCP company dinners today. I miss their food sometimes, though I'd rather work for Hiroki in Atlanta as his assistant than be the office manager in Savannah."

"Yeah, we each fill a niche, and ideally we do what God has gifted us to do."

Even as she said it, Maggie wondered if she was taking her own advice. She loved working at the church and being in ministry every day. Thanks to her personal messy emotions, she had sent in her resignation and would be starting a new job in the marketing department of a resort. Sure, it was Christian owned, but it was still a commercial company and not a church.

What had God gifted her to do?

As she was thinking about it, they somehow reached the last lamppost. Maggie had lost track of time.

Oblivious to her thoughts, Alden continued his brief history of Chef Forsythia McDevitt.

"Forsythia hit a career ceiling at Piper's Place. She wanted to be the chef de cuisine, but there was already one there."

Maggie nodded. "Chef Piper herself."

"Exactly. When our Midtown chef retired, I told Forsythia about the job opening. She sent in her résumé—totally overqualified with great recommendations from Chef Piper. Of course, she got the job when she didn't care if her salary at church was lower than that at a regular restaurant." Then Alden paused. "Why do you ask?"

"A friend of mine is interested in her."

"Really?" Mischief in his elfin eyes.

Maggie knew she had spoken too much. She busied herself disentangling the strings of lights. When they put them away last year, they had just dumped them all into this box.

Alden came to help her. "How about this? Let's go out to dinner, the four of us. Casual like. We can see how it goes with your friend and Forsythia."

He ended it there, but Maggie could almost guess that he could have added "and us." If he had, it'd be the end of their friendship. It seemed that Alden was wise not to step where he shouldn't.

Not at this time, anyhow.

"You mean you'd invite Forsythia to dinner and I'd invite my friend?" Maggie asked.

"That works too."

"How would you ask Forsythia?"

"I'll tell her that I've got a blind date for her."

"Without knowing who my friend is?" Maggie asked.

"I trust you. We're friends, aren't we?"

Only friends. Maggie didn't say it aloud.

"It's just dinner. No big deal. If it makes you feel better, we'll go Dutch. Let's do it for your friend's sake."

For Levi's sake.

"Hmm. I guess that's fine. When?" Maggie didn't want to disclose that she had a time crunch. Technically, her last day wasn't until December 31, but church offices were closed in the last week of December, and she'd planned to use those days to move from Georgia to Florida.

"Whenever you want." Alden gave her a quick smile.

"The sooner, the better. Before Christmas, preferably."

"In a hurry, are we?"

"My friend is." Or maybe Maggie was too. Perhaps once Levi was taken, Maggie could move on.

Move on?

It felt impossible at this time, but nothing was impossible with God, after all.

Chapter Four

*L*evi almost forgot to pray for God's perfect will as he waited impatiently for Saturday to come. By Wednesday he was too anxious to focus on work at the warehouse.

With all the overtime he'd had, he left work early and picked up Maggie from Midtown Chapel at five o'clock on the dot and they went to a nearby mall to get him some new clothes he could wear to the Singles Ministry Christmas dinner.

It was going to be a catered dinner, and he didn't want to look underdressed. He wanted to impress Forsythia, most of all, since the chef had been to formal events and had no doubt acquired an impeccable taste.

But this party wasn't that formal. That was why he needed Maggie's help.

They walked toward a designer store on the second floor of the mall, and Levi was hurrying Maggie along. He stepped back and grabbed her hand and pulled her forward.

Maggie twisted her hand out of Levi's. "I gather that you want us to get back to church for supper, right?"

"Since you're my shopping assistant today, I'll take you to dinner at the food court."

"Will we still make it to the midweek service?"

"I think I can get us back there by seven."

Maggie followed Levi as he walked among the racks of jackets.

"What about this one?" Levi pointed to a wool blazer. It was charcoal.

"Don't you have a charcoal jacket at home?" Maggie ran her fingers over some other jackets nearby.

"I do."

"So why buy another one?"

"My jacket is old."

"So? The dinner is only for two hours."

"Right, but I don't want Forsythia to see me looking run-down."

Maggie turned away and Levi couldn't see her

face. He stepped toward her. She blinked. Were those tears in her eyes?

"Are you bored?" Levi asked. "Was that a yawn I detected?"

"No." Maggie sniffled.

"Coming down with a cold?" Levi leaned toward her face.

Maggie stepped back. Started checking the labels and tags on a row of sport coats. Then she pulled a black-and-cream herringbone sport coat off the rack. "How about this? You don't have one in this color and this might make you stand out."

Levi wasn't sure if he wanted to stand out. He just wanted to get a date with Forsythia.

"If you think that will help me, Matchmaker Maggie." Levi took the jacket from her. "Is this my size?"

"Yes."

"You know me well. I'll go try it on." Levi looked around for signs of the fitting rooms.

"Wait. You need to pair it with something. A vest or a nice sweater."

"Let's do a vest. What color do you think I should wear?" Levi followed her to a row of vests.

"Burgundy looks good." She picked one his size and lifted the vest against the coat that Levi held.

"Nice." Levi smiled. "Again, you know me

well, Maggie. You know my favorite color, my size, and what works well together."

"You can thank Malachi for that. I had to help him shop too."

Levi wondered if Maggie had helped more men than just her brother and himself. He didn't want to ask. They didn't have much time for chit-chatting.

"Oh wait." Maggie's eyes widened as she showed Levi the price tag. "This vest is pure cash-mere and costs three hundred dollars."

"It's all right."

"You're dipping into your savings just to get dressed up for Saturday? What if she says no?"

"I hope she says yes to lunch with me."

Maggie didn't reply to that. "You're also going to need some sort of shirt to go inside the vest. Maybe just wear one of your buttoned-down shirts? And jeans? Then you'll save money."

Levi nodded. "Good idea, Mags. I need to have something left over to pay for lunch with her."

Maggie looked away again.

What's the matter with this woman?

Maggie pointed toward a sign on the wall. "Fitting rooms are over there. I'll wait."

"Where?"

"I guess I'll go to the women's section and look around."

"I'll find you there."

On the way to the fitting rooms, Levi picked up a couple of new dress shirts to try out. Yeah, he had a lot of shirts at home, but he wanted new clothes. He decided to get a new pair of jeans too. He wasn't too picky about jeans, as long as they were stretchable.

Maybe wearing all new clothes was an overkill, but he really wanted to look good on Saturday. If he couldn't talk to Forsythia and make any progress with her, then he'd be out something like fifteen hundred dollars.

He walked out of the stall fully dressed in his new attire. He wanted to show Maggie how he looked.

He found her in the women's section, staring at a full-length plaid skirt. She gasped at the price tag.

"You like it?" Levi asked.

"Not the price." Maggie stepped back, not looking at him. Levi felt warm thinking that Maggie recognized his voice. "I need to save money for the m... Ah, I can't spend it."

"Save money for what?" Levi asked.

Maggie turned around and stared at him. No words.

Levi knew not to press further. It wasn't like they were an item. Maggie didn't have to tell him everything. No reason for her to. They were best friends, yes, but sometimes Levi didn't need to know what she didn't want to talk about.

Lately, Maggie had been pensive and quiet. Maybe in the last month or so. Sure, Levi had talked to her, and Maggie sounded normal. She smiled and chatted with him as per usual.

However, she seemed to have better and brighter conversations with Alden, for example, rather than with him. Levi recalled the workday at the Village community center on Saturday when Maggie and Alden worked well together.

Other than telling Levi about Alden's idea for a double date night, Maggie had said little else. She had somehow given Levi the impression that she was holding something back.

What, precisely?

Maybe the pressure of work had gotten to her. Maybe it was the fact that Midtown Chapel had split up her job into two, and hired a new ministry assistant for Midtown Village with a new manager and all. That had left her with half her usual plate of work, concentrating her focus on simply being the ministry assistant at the women's ministry. Perhaps being in the office at the church basement all day was not something Maggie wanted to do anymore.

"Wow." Maggie walked around Levi. "This works. Good idea to wear jeans with this. You won't look overdressed."

"Thanks. Glad you like it. You helped out a lot."

"Mmm. A new shirt too." Maggie pointed. "Don't you have enough shirts at home?"

"I just wanted everything to be new... Well, except the socks and boxers."

"TMI, Levi." Maggie covered her face with her hands. "Even best friends don't have to talk about certain things."

Levi realized that too. Maybe he considered Maggie like one of his buddies, someone with whom he wasn't shy.

Maggie glanced at her watch. "You might want to change out of all that and go pay for the clothes because we have to go. We have half an hour to eat if we want to make it back to church in downtown traffic."

"One sec. If you want this skirt, I'll buy it." Levi said. "Consider it my Christmas gift for you."

"That's sweet." Maggie pointed to the price tag. "You might want to see the price before you decide to buy me things."

"I'm not going to look at it. I want you to have

it. You deserve all the love." Levi didn't earn much as the warehouse manager, but he'd saved up a lot, thanks to a small inheritance from Uncle Melvin and Aunt Marie after they had passed away within months of each other.

"If you want to give me a Christmas present…" Maggie started to say.

"Say it."

"Then you might consider donating the equivalent amount to mission work."

That was the Maggie that Levi knew. Always putting others ahead of herself. Perhaps she had learned it while growing up as a missionary kid, although her parents did mission work stateside, though in the last few years they had traveled from country to country.

After college, Maggie's brother had followed their parents' footsteps to become a missionary overseas, while Maggie worked in a church to this day. It seemed to Levi that she would always be a woman in ministry.

"I'm not surprised you said that, Mags." Levi put all his clothes over one arm. He reached for the price tag of the imported wool skirt that Maggie had liked minutes ago.

Unbelievable.

Yeah, he was too quick to give, but this was Maggie, whom he considered to be the best among all his friends. If he could give the world to Maggie, he would.

Levi was a man of his word, so there goes nineteen hundred dollars plus a few cents.

"I'll round up this amount and give it to the mission agency of your choice," Levi said.

"You're so generous. You can always take back your word, you know. I won't hold it against you."

"No, no." Pride had spoken.

"Then how about giving it to our church mission fund? It will be equally shared among all the missionaries."

"Good idea." Levi made quick work of it. He logged onto the Midtown Chapel church app and donated two thousand dollars, designating them to be distributed to the missionaries whom the church supported. No, he wasn't super rich or anything, but that money would come out of his savings.

"Wow, Levi. Thank you." Maggie's eyes were red again.

Levi studied Maggie's face. "You don't happen to have pink eye, do you?"

"Ah no. Dust or allergies. Don't worry about me." Her voice cracked.

"You miss your brother in Florida and your parents overseas." Levi hadn't met Maggie's parents, but they were near retirement age after a number of years of missionary work.

Maggie laughed. "You say the most random things, Levi. Again, no, I don't have the pink eye. Yes, my parents are always on my mind, but I wasn't thinking about Malachi or family either. I was just thinking that instead of buying this skirt for me to wear a few times only in the winter months, it would be better if you gave the gift to our missionaries who are always looking for additional support. And then you went and made that happen. I'm so happy, but I hate to even suggest it because it's your money, not mine."

"Don't worry. If Uncle Melvin and Aunt Marie were alive, they would be happy to donate the money to mission work." He was sure of it.

Maggie grabbed his arm. "But I don't want you to feel bad that you splurged on the coat and vest. You wear them well."

"I'm glad you approve. I hope Forsythia likes the coat too."

Levi expected Maggie to smile, but she did not. She barely nodded.

Levi wasn't sure if he should read anything in her non-expression, but once again, he felt that she was holding something back from him.

Would their relationship change should he start dating Forsythia, if it ever came to that?

He expected Maggie to be happy for him.

Surely she wasn't jealous of Forsythia. After all, Maggie had been the one who had asked Alden if he knew Forsythia. As a result, Alden had suggested a double date night.

Oh wait.

Alden.

Levi wasn't sure if he wanted Maggie to be Alden's date at all. No, no.

Things seemed to be getting complicated. Levi wanted to protect Maggie from Alden, but he also wanted that dinner with Forsythia.

Could he have both?

Chapter Five

For the first time since Levi met Forsythia, he saw her smile at him. Or she might be smiling at Alden, who was standing beside him in the glass-enclosed rooftop restaurant. Levi couldn't be sure.

In any case, progress had been made this evening at the singles Christmas dinner, although Levi didn't want to credit Alden for it. When Maggie showed up, he'd thank her for it by reminding her that he had donated two thousand dollars to the mission fund at church.

Trust Maggie to ground him in what mattered. He felt good giving money to mission work, to support ministries local and abroad.

When Maggie had reminded him to "pray about it" to be certain that it was what he was personally convicted to do, Levi wondered if he was backsliding from the faith, having spent an enormous amount of mental and emotional energy thinking about getting close to Forsythia, albeit without changing his career to food science or something kitchen-related just to be in her world.

Forsythia seemed to be a mirage.

On the other hand, Maggie was real. She was the stable Christian friend in his life. Levi knew he could trust Maggie to always talk with him honestly and as objectively as she could, without sugarcoating the truth or justifying lies. She was straightforward.

Yet, something had been bothering her of late.

Levi made a mental note to ask her as soon as she arrived at the dinner. He glanced at the clock on his phone. "She's late."

"Who?" Alden asked.

Levi didn't think he spoke that loudly. He was mumbling to himself. "Maggie."

"I've saved her a seat." Alden said it so casual-like, as though he and Maggie had been friends for ages. "If she doesn't make it until dessert is served, I'll save her some. She likes anything chocolate."

Now why would Alden say that? How well did he know Maggie?

"Is that right?" Forsythia said. "Maggie is in

such good shape that I didn't think she indulged in sweet stuff."

"She told me that she prefers dark chocolate, but when it comes to Christmas, she'd eat anything chocolate, regardless." Alden smirked.

Levi had nothing to say. Actually, he wasn't sure if Maggie was such a chocoholic. Maggie loved hot cocoa year round, but chocolate itself wasn't on top of her list. At Christmas, she loved cookies—although she couldn't bake them herself to save her life—but did Maggie like "anything chocolate" as a matter of preference?

All right. Perhaps he was overthinking this. Levi looked away for a minute to gather his thoughts. He felt nervous in front of Forsythia, but found himself thinking of how to counter anything Alden said about Maggie.

Something was off.

Around them, singles from church and their plus ones were mingling with one another as they tasted the hors d'oeuvres. Most of them were in attire dressier than church on Sunday mornings, but not formal.

Levi's eyes roamed about the restaurant near the entrance.

Where is Maggie?

He had last seen her on Wednesday after church when they went to the mall together. For the next two days after that, Maggie had been busy in meetings about the future direction of Midtown Village with the addition of the plot of land nearby. Pastor Kim presided over the meeting, but Maggie went because of her vast knowledge of the Village, having been the previous women's ministry director's right-hand woman—back when the women's ministry was in charge of the Village since the city ministry had primarily served single mothers and their children.

Maggie canceled her plans to bake cookies on Saturday, so Levi ended up not going to her house to prevent her from burning down the kitchen.

The singles ministry pastor took the microphone and welcomed everyone to the dinner. "I want to thank RYUCP for sponsoring this event and to Skye's the Limit for catering tonight."

Everyone clapped.

Still no sign of Maggie. Levi reached for his phone and texted her. *Where are you?*

"I'm going to make a few announcements as you make your way to your tables, and then I'll ask my lovely wife to come up here and pray over our meal tonight."

Alden tapped Levi's shoulder, leaned toward his ear to whisper: "I saved you a seat next to Forsythia."

Levi was supposed to be elated, but he felt nothing.

Right now he wanted to know why Maggie hadn't shown up. Maybe she had car trouble. Maybe she had been in a wreck. Maybe it was a fender bender and she was waiting for her car to be towed. That beat-up old car of hers couldn't last two hours on the streets of Atlanta. Good thing she lived near church so she was at least close to work.

Atlanta traffic is so bad.

Uh-oh. Maybe Maggie was in the hospital right now, fighting for her life.

The more he thought about it, the worse it got.

Calm down, Levi.

What did Maggie always say when things seemed out of control? Sometimes things seemed difficult at work or at the Village, where residents sometimes arrived carrying baggage filled with grief and despair. Sometimes it was easy for church workers to take on themselves the burdens of others, thereby stressing out themselves.

Maggie had told him something he never forgot. "Trusting God begins with surrendering our thoughts to God. All of it, including our imaginative thoughts that might not be biblically based.

If I keep imagining the worst, then I may forget that God is still the sovereign ruler over all."

Then she would remind herself of Bible verses, including 2 Corinthians 10:3-6. As if it was necessary for his own sanity, he opened his Bible app and searched for the verse, one of Maggie's favorites.

> *For though we walk in the flesh, we do not war according to the flesh. For the weapons of our warfare are not carnal but mighty in God for pulling down strongholds, casting down arguments and every high thing that exalts itself against the knowledge of God, bringing every thought into captivity to the obedience of Christ, and being ready to punish all disobedience when your obedience is fulfilled.*

Maggie often reminded him to pray about everything. "Nothing is beyond God."

Levi realized that he was overly worried about Maggie. Why, though? Had he started to treat Maggie more than just a best buddy, but perhaps as his sister or more? He wasn't sure. All he knew right now was that he wanted Maggie to be okay.

Levi checked his messages again. Radio silence.

Lord Jesus, please. I don't know where Maggie is. She's not answering her messages. I will call her in a minute. Where is she? I am worried about her, so please take my every thought captive to the obedience of Christ. The more I think about her being missing, the worse my thoughts get.

Levi went outside the restaurant so he could make a phone call. It was a useless exercise since Maggie simply didn't pick up. He left a brief message for her, trying not to sound panicky.

He regretted not carpooling with Maggie this evening, but she had texted him on Friday afternoon sometime to tell him not to because she didn't want to depend on him for transportation home after dinner. She also might have to leave the dinner party early, although she didn't say why.

Friday afternoon had been the last time Levi had communicated with Maggie at all. After that, no text or voicemail from her. Not that it was unusual. Sometimes they were both busy and didn't call or message each other for days.

He returned to the restaurant and saw Alden waving to him from a corner table. Alden pointed to two empty seats between himself and Forsythia.

When Levi got closer, Alden put a palm down on the seat next to his. "I'm saving this seat for Maggie. That one is yours."

"That one" was the seat next to Forsythia.

Wasn't this when Levi should feel a tingling in

his chest because he was finally sitting next to his elusive dream date?

He felt nothing.

As though his chase was coming to a close and there was no medal to speak of. Perhaps he was in the wrong race to begin with.

Wrong race?

Wasn't Chef Forsythia McDevitt the best prospect for a girlfriend? Sure, Levi had been watching her from afar—she in the kitchen side and he on the other side of the buffet line at Wednesday night supper.

Perhaps he had been living with an illusion.

Perhaps his dreams had been interrupted by reality: Maggie.

He sat down. To his right was his dream date, Forsythia. To his left was an empty seat reserved for his best friend, Maggie.

Levi took a deep breath.

If I made a mistake, Lord, can I backtrack now?

Forsythia was busy talking to a man seated on the other side of her. Levi didn't know who that person was and didn't care.

Maggie's seat was still empty. Next to it, Alden tapped on his phone.

"You happen to know where Maggie is?" Levi asked.

"I'm trying to find out." Alden lifted his phone. "I texted her. No reply."

Of course Alden had Maggie's phone number. They worked together on the Village tiny homes. Eventually, Maggie might not need Alden's number because Erika was taking over Maggie's job at the Village.

"Do you think she's sick?" Alden asked.

"Why do you say that?"

"Hope she didn't get food poisoning from last night."

Last night? What was Alden talking about? "What about last night?"

"Oh, we finished our meeting late, so we went out to dinner at a seafood restaurant. Maggie ordered grouper and thought it smelled, and she didn't like her fish to smell, but she ate it anyway. I had grouper too but I'm fine."

We?

"What about the others?" Levi asked.

"Just me and her. I asked my colleagues but they were too tired to go."

Just like Maggie. She hated to waste food. Levi had told her that very thing the last time she got sick eating some fishcake that smelled. If the dish looked or smelled suspicious, she shouldn't have eaten it. If she wanted fresher seafood, she should move to the coast somewhere, rather than eat at restaurants where the fresh catch was flown in.

How many times do I have to tell her?

Levi shook his head. The first course was being served, so Levi assumed the pastor had said a blessing over the food while he had been outside in the hallway trying to contact Maggie.

He stared at the salad, and decided he couldn't sit here and eat dinner while Maggie was probably at home with a stomach ache or worse.

He left his seat and swiped his phone, checking Google Maps for the nearest open pharmacy or grocery store so he could pick up some medicine for his poor friend.

Levi arrived at Maggie's house near Midtown Village, but no one answered the doorbell. It was 8:17 p.m. and he had arrived later than expected. After his stop at the pharmacy aisle in the Publix grocery store, he went home to get the spare house key that Maggie had let him keep. His house was a good twenty minutes away from Maggie's.

Still, he had brought with him a box of over-the-counter anti-diarrheal medication and a dozen bottles of Gatorade, just in case.

In his mind, he tried to figure out which twenty-four-hour urgent care center to take Maggie to if it was something worse than eating bad food.

To begin with, he wasn't sure what had happened to her.

Once again, he felt himself overthinking this.

He asked God to forgive him and correct his thinking. "Capture my thoughts, Lord."

He rang the doorbell again.

No answer.

He started to panic a little. If he used the spare key, would Maggie accuse him of breaking and entering? Well, why would she? After all, she was the one who had given him the spare key.

For emergency situations.

Like this one?

She could be dead inside. My best friend!

Levi unlocked the door and rushed into the house—

And nearly collided with a stack of giant moving boxes by the door.

Boxes, boxes everywhere.

Not just any boxes, but moving boxes.

"What in the world?" He made his way through the maze of boxes until he found the living room.

Maggie was asleep on the couch in her flannel pajamas. A blanket was half on her and half on the floor.

Before Levi could check if Maggie was alive,

she turned and continued sleeping, her hair all askew on the pillow.

She had beautiful brown hair but that wasn't the point now.

Maggie was alive.

"Thank You, Jesus."

Levi put the bag of OTC medicine and Gatorade bottles on the scratched-up coffee table.

Then he took off his sport coat, sat on the recliner on the other side of the coffee table, kicked off his shoes, and checked his phone. He wasn't sure how long he was at it before the recliner felt too comfortable and he couldn't keep his eyes open.

Chapter Six

*I*n the middle of the night, Levi opened his eyes when he heard the toilet flushing. Above him, the ceiling lights were off, but distant hallway lights enabled him to somewhat see in the gray haze.

His brain felt mushy and his muscles were sore. The recliner wasn't exactly his own bed, and he really needed eight hours of uninterrupted sleep each night.

He felt something soft on his arms, and realized it felt something like a chenille throw. He didn't remember falling asleep, nor did he remember covering himself up.

Pattering of house slippers made him turn toward the hallway. Maggie came out of the bathroom, clutching her stomach.

His leg muscles pushed down at the leg rest and he sprung out of the recliner. "You okay, Mags?"

She barely nodded. She was wearing an old tee shirt and a pair of flannel pajama pants. And she walked slowly. On the way to the living room, she flicked on the lights. "Why are you here?"

The fact that she wasn't surprised that Levi had entered her house using her spare key made Levi guess that she had been the one who'd placed the chenille throw over him.

"You were a no-show at the singles dinner party. Do you know where your phone is?"

"I don't know."

Levi decided to find it later. "I was so worried when you didn't answer my texts and phone calls."

"Well, I ate something bad yesterday and I've been sick all day long. I was either in my bedroom or in the bathroom."

"I bought you some Gatorade." He knew that wasn't enough. "Let's go to urgent care."

Maggie made her way to the couch and slowly sat down. She pointed to a box on the table. "Got some medicine."

Levi checked. It was the same medicine he'd bought earlier this evening.

"Two tablets left." He read the expiration date. Still a few weeks to go.

He took the medicine he'd bought out of the shopping bag and placed the unopened box on the coffee table near a plastic bottled water that was almost empty.

However, Maggie didn't look well. He didn't want her to just take over-the-counter medicine. What if her stomach ache was something else?

"You look terrible," Levi said. "Get dressed. Let's go."

Maggie shook her head. She puffed up her bedroom pillow which she'd been using on the couch. She flipped it over and rested her head on it. "How's dinner?"

Levi sat at her feet. Her socks were falling off her feet, so he adjusted them for her. "I left early."

"You shouldn't have. Alden said he made sure to seat Forsythia next to you. You missed the opportunity to get to know her." Maggie reached for a blanket.

Forsythia? Levi didn't want to talk about her.

Right now, Maggie was more important.

He caught himself thinking that. "Are you cold? Should I turn up the thermostat?"

"No need. I'm fine. Might be time for me to take more meds." She stretched her hand out toward the box.

Levi saw the near-empty bottled water on the

table. "Don't you have filtered water? The plastic bottle might leach chemicals into the water."

"I usually boil water but I don't feel like it."

Levi reached for a Gatorade bottle on the other side of the table. "Have you just been going to the bathroom or did you also throw up?"

"Both."

That alarmed Levi. "I still think we need to take you to urgent care."

"I don't want to go."

"Says the sick person. You know, I've often wondered how sickness affects decision making."

Maggie ignored him. "Will you also make me chicken soup and hot herbal tea? My tummy hurts."

"Yes, ma'am. If you want me to, I can make you some tea now." Levi knew where the kitchen was. He had been here numerous times in the last three years.

He felt at home in Maggie's house, which she shared with her brother. The Jacobs family had bought the house together—with some inheritance money after their great-grandpa passed away—so that when Malachi and their parents came home on furlough, they could stay here. There were four bedrooms in all.

Levi had met Malachi, but not his parents.

"I have cans of chicken soup in the pantry," Maggie said.

"If you want me to cook chicken soup for you, I can do it from scratch." Levi glanced in the direction where he could usually see a clock on the wall, but now there was a stack of boxes in the way.

He wanted to ask about the boxes, but this didn't seem to be the right time.

He checked the phone in his pocket. It was almost three in the morning. Yikes.

"So you're going to cook for me?" Maggie chuckled. "You're like a fill-in older brother. Malachi also cooks chicken soup from scratch. He makes the stock first. It takes forever to have just one bowl."

Older brother?

Up until the day before, Levi hadn't thought much about his relationship with Maggie, but after being worried about her last evening, he wondered if there was something more between them.

They had known each other for only three years, but he felt that he was closer to her than her brother was. They talked about challenges at work and in the ministry a lot. They spent a lot of time together. Ate out together. Attended church activities together.

No way they were only best friends.

The only thing he hadn't done was to… kiss her.

"Thank you for the meds and Gatorade." Maggie's voice interrupted his thoughts.

"No problem. I suggest you rest at home in the morning and livestream the church service."

Maggie nodded.

"I'll fill out the sermon notes and email you."

More nods.

"You can go now, Levi. What would people at church say if they find out you slept here at my house?"

"Frankly, I don't care. God knows there's nothing going on between us."

"Still, we have no witnesses, just you and me."

"We're best friends."

"Even more so."

Levi sighed. "All right, before I go, I'll find your phone so you can have it near you in case you need to make an emergency call."

Even as he said that, Levi felt reluctant to leave. What if something happened to Maggie between now and the time he returned after church?

Aunt Marie had always said that instead of worrying needlessly, he should pray. "Let's pray before I go."

Maggie closed her eyes.

Levi began to pray. "Heavenly Father, thank You for giving us life. We come to You now because Mags is sick. Make her well. Give her rest. Strengthen her body to overcome this. Protect her henceforth from bad food. I wish I were there with her because I'd have told her not to eat the fish if it smelled bad. But I wasn't there. Forgive me, Lord. I failed to protect her. I was so busy with my own selfish needs..."

Needs? They were more like wants.

He drew a deep breath. Jumbled thoughts made him unable to say another word. Had he lost his way? He'd been singularly focused on pursuing Forsythia. She seemed like a dead end. In the process, he'd neglected his best friend.

A hand touched his arm.

Levi opened his eyes. "I'm still praying. Lie down."

Maggie frowned. "I ate the fish. You didn't. Stop feeling guilty."

"Stop interrupting me when I pray."

"I'm sorry. You weren't speaking for a while. I thought..." Maggie put her head back down on the pillow. "Go on."

Levi sighed. Closed his eyes. "Lord Jesus, please heal Mags completely. In Your holy name I pray. Amen."

"Amen. Thank You, Jesus." Maggie smiled.

"And thank you, Levi, for praying for me and for coming over to check on me."

A little glimpse of Maggie had returned. She was always appreciative of anything Levi did for her. A small prayer here. A visit there. Maggie noticed.

Yet she had withheld information from him. Behind the couch were more various sized boxes stacked up. He couldn't miss seeing them. "Why am I seeing moving boxes everywhere?"

At first Maggie was quiet. Then slowly she said, "I was going to tell you next week, but I guess you found out. I've handed in my resignation at Midtown. After Christmas, I'm moving to Lakeside to live near my parents, whom you know have just retired from the mission field."

"This is so sudden. Have you prayed about it?" Levi asked.

"It's best for us all." Maggie felt sad, but she had to do this. "You can still come see us if you want. Only seven hours. Like driving around Atlanta two or three times. No big deal."

Levi nodded. "Your parents must be very happy that you're moving closer to them."

He felt resigned to the separation. As though there was nothing he could do about it. Maggie was moving away.

"What about this house?" Levi looked up at the ceiling and all around.

"My parents want to sell the house, so we have to clear out." Maggie pressed a palm on her tummy. It was aching again. "I've been packing what I can, but the movers are coming twice. On the eighteenth, they will haul away my parents' stuff they left behind here the last forty years. On the twenty-eighth, they'll come back to move my things."

"You're not packing alone, are you?"

"Since I haven't told anyone but Mrs. Kim that I'm leaving, I wasn't able to ask anyone to help me, but there's not a lot to do, really. I'm just packing mementos and books and breakables I don't want anyone to touch. The movers will do everything."

"Must be expensive."

"Well, the owner of Lakeside Resort is Tally's grandmother, and she's decided to pay to move Mom and Dad's stuff. I'll pay for my own move because I don't want to bother anyone this Christmas season."

"You forgot me, Mags." Levi didn't know what to think. "How quickly you've forgotten your best friend who's coming this afternoon to cook chicken soup for you and help you pack."

"I do love your chicken soup."

"Yeah, you told me. To the moon and back."

Maggie chuckled. "Truth be told, I can eat canned soup. No big deal. Save you time and take Sunday afternoon off."

"I'd rather spend it with you—"

She gasped, covered her mouth, threw back her blanket, and ran to the bathroom.

Levi heard the door slam shut.

"She's still sick and won't see a doctor. How can I leave her alone?" He swiped his phone and logged in. Searched Google Maps for the nearest twenty-four-seven urgent care.

Hmm. Fifteen minutes away. If he put a bucket in his truck, they might make it.

Maggie dragged herself back to the couch. Before she sat down, Levi stood up. "Girl, I'm taking you to urgent care right now. Go get dressed."

"No."

"You want me to dress you? I can." Levi made it like he was walking toward her bedroom.

She stopped him. "You wouldn't dare. I'll tell my brother."

Levi smiled. "Then get dressed yourself."

He paused. "On second thought, just go as you are. You have a goose down coat that goes to your ankle. That's enough."

"You want me to wear pajamas to the doctor's office?"

"Why not? You're sick."

Maggie made a face. Pushed Levi aside. "Give me two minutes."

Levi got himself a drink of water from the refrigerator. On the door were magnets holding up family photos. Two were dated and showed Maggie and Malachi when they were kids, playing firefighters. One seemed new and showed Maggie's parents at some castle in Europe. It was a group shot with two other people.

Must be nice to still have parents. Levi's father had died a long time ago, when Levi was still a teenager. Dad had fallen overboard at the offshore oil rig where he worked. His body had never been found.

Years later, Levi's mother died of leukemia. An only child, he went to live with Uncle Melvin and Aunt Marie in Savannah, Georgia, until he went to college.

He had been on his own since.

The bedroom door opened. It creaked a little. Levi made a mental note to oil the hinges.

Maggie stepped out. She had upgraded from pajamas to a sweater and sweatpants. Her goose down coat was in her hands.

Sometimes Levi slept in his sweatpants, so he

wasn't sure why Maggie couldn't just wear her pajamas to urgent care.

"You know I can drive myself," Maggie said.

"I know. But I'm here, Mags. Let me take care of you." Levi helped Maggie with her coat.

"Why are you so nice to me?"

"Aren't we best buddies? If I were sick, wouldn't you do the same?"

"Sure."

Levi remembered something. "Just so you know, I had to use your spare key to get in last night when you didn't answer the door."

"That's why I gave you the key. In case of emergencies, come rescue me. If I lock myself out of the house, come help me." Maggie's voice cracked. "You're the best man, Levi—besides my brother and Dad, of course."

Family.

Or family zoned?

"Do you have your phone?" Levi asked.

Maggie checked her purse. "Not here. Not sure where I put it."

Levi swiped his own phone and called Maggie's phone. He couldn't hear a thing.

"It might have run out of battery," Maggie said. "I meant to charge it."

"Haven't I told you to charge it every night? Then you won't forget to charge it."

"Oh, Bossy Levi speaks." Maggie was about to sit down on the couch when she gripped her tummy and ran back into her bedroom to the bathroom.

Levi checked the tracker app on his phone. After Maggie had misplaced her phone at church one day, she agreed to let Levi install a tracker on her phone.

The tracker told Levi that the phone was in the sunroom. He made his way through the maze of packing boxes to the sunroom. These boxes were starting to bother him. They were marked with different locations of the house. Kitchen, bathroom, hallway, library, closet. Where was Maggie going?

One thing at a time.

First, he had to find Maggie's phone.

In a far corner of the sunroom was a small writing desk with a lamp on top. In the daytime, it overlooked the same herb garden he could see from the kitchen window.

He recognized that writing desk. It used to belong to Aunt Marie. When they moved to the Savannah Senior Living Resort on Tybee Island, they had to downsize their condominium. Aunt Marie offered her old writing desk to Levi, and he accepted it.

A few years later when Levi started working at

the Midtown Chapel warehouse and became fast friends with Maggie and her brother, Malachi, he knew he wanted to give them the desk as a sign of their enduring friendship.

On top of the writing desk was a closed journal on top of a Bible. Next to that was Maggie's phone. Levi didn't open the journal because it had Maggie's name etched on the cover. Privacy mattered to him.

When he lifted up the phone, there was a small pink Post-It note underneath, stuck to the blotter desktop.

He didn't mean to read the apparent note-to-self, but there it was, in Maggie's best cursive handwriting. They were words that Levi didn't want to see or hear.

Say goodbye to Levi.

"What does that mean? Where is she going?" Levi mumbled to himself as he looked for the phone's charging cable. He found it in the small front drawer of the desk. It was hot pink in color. He knew it wasn't Maggie's favorite color, but he suspected that she had probably bought it because the color would pop out when she looked for it.

Maggie was practical like that.

What about saying goodbye to him? Why must

she leave him? Even if he were dating Forsythia—or anyone else—why couldn't he still be best friends with Maggie?

Next to the table was a small trash can with a liner in it. Levi picked it up and took it with him.

When he returned to the living room, Maggie was sobbing into her blanket. She was facing the back cushion, and her shoulders were shuddering.

Levi put the phone and small trash can down and went to Maggie.

The couch seat was wide and could fit two adults side by side. Levi sat down at the edge of it and put his hand on her shoulder.

She stiffened. Wiped her eyes and went silent.

"Mags," Levi said softly.

No reply.

"Maggie." Levi tried again.

Slowly, she turned to face him. Her eyes were red. "I hate being sick."

"I know." He rubbed her arm.

"It's three in the morning and if we go to urgent care and then to the pharmacy, we won't be back for a while. And then I'd only get a few hours of sleep and I may have to miss church this morning. I hate missing church."

"I know. We can livestream. Make technology work."

"We?" Maggie's eyes widened. "You're not

sick. You need to physically go to church if at all possible."

"Maybe I should stay with you." Levi felt that Maggie needed someone to be with her.

"No need. I only ate some bad fish. I'll get over this." Maggie's voice toughened. "Let's go to urgent care so I can get over this. Then you can go to church for us."

For us?

Was there such a thing?

"Don't miss church on account of me."

This was the Maggie whom Levi knew. She was vulnerable every now and then, but she was never lost. In spite of interruptions to her daily life, she remained steadfast in the things she knew she must do. Levi supposed that kept her grounded when work and life became chaotic.

"One sec." Levi picked up the trash can.

"What are you doing?"

"Putting a new liner on this trash can. We're going to take it with us. Don't want you to throw up all over my pickup truck." Levi found a clean liner in the kitchen pantry and swapped out the liner.

He came back and helped Maggie on her feet.

The whole time, the words that Maggie had written on the note bothered him.

Say goodbye to Levi.

What did Maggie mean by that?

"Where's my phone?" Maggie picked up her phone from the coffee table. It was out of battery.

"You can charge it up in my truck," Levi said.

"Okay." She handed her phone to him.

Levi put on his sport coat.

"Is that all you have? It's cold out." Maggie pointed to the coat closet by the door. "Malachi left his jackets in there. He doesn't need them in Florida. See if one fits you."

Levi found an insulated jacket that fit him and hung up his coat on the same hanger. "Do you and your brother only wear goose down coats?"

"Yeah. You know we don't like cold weather. Why Malachi jumped on the first opportunity to move to Florida."

In the truck, Levi used Maggie's extension cord to plug her phone into his dashboard charger.

As soon as the juice reached the phone, Levi saw that Maggie had missed messages from him, but also... Alden. He couldn't see what the messages were, but it said right there on her pop-up notifications that Alden had texted her fifteen times.

Fifteen! What on earth? What for?

Levi had never been jealous of anyone before until now.

Wait a minute.

Why would he be jealous of Alden? It had been his fault that Maggie was sick now. Alden had taken her to eat seafood on Friday night, and that was how Maggie got food poisoning or something.

So yeah, why would Levi be jealous of Alden? The latter did Maggie no good.

As for Levi and Maggie, their relationship had been only platonic in the last three years. It had gone well for them since they were both single and dateless.

Now Alden had slipped into the picture and attempted to ruin Levi's view.

For the first time in their friendship, Levi began to realize that perhaps Maggie was more than just a friend to him. He wanted Maggie to himself, and not share her with Alden.

Oh…that came out all wrong.

But the fact remained that Maggie was special to Levi. She might not have been, but she was now. He couldn't imagine life without Maggie.

No, he didn't want to say goodbye to her. At all.

Why hadn't he noticed that before?

Chapter Seven

$\mathcal{M}$aggie woke up at ten thirty and stayed there on the couch, watching beams of sun rays stream into her living room. She'd only had five hours of sleep, but didn't feel too groggy. For the first time in twenty four hours, she didn't have to sprint to the bathroom.

Her tummy felt better, but she wasn't over it.

Still, she thanked God that it turned out that she only had a mild case of food poisoning from the bad grouper she had eaten on Friday night. The doctor at the urgent care prescribed her over-the-counter medication, if she needed it, and plenty of fluid and rest.

After the doctor's visit, Levi took Maggie to the nearest Walgreens to get her prescriptions. By the time they got home it was five in the morning.

Levi decided not to stay, so he drove all the way home to Dunwoody. Promised to take notes for her at the second service and come back after church to cook chicken soup for her.

"Lord, I have to get well."

This upcoming week was going to be terribly busy for her as she expected to finish handing over all her Midtown Village work to Erika Song.

Thank God she wasn't involved in the annual Christmas play at church, or else she'd be stressed out from doing too much.

Already, packing up the house to prepare for her move to Florida had been a chore. She spent half her time crying whenever she saw something that Levi had given her. A crazy Christmas sweatshirt here, a birthday gift there. Even a souvenir from their mission trip together to the Bahamas made her cry.

The last three years had been filled with too much Levi.

It would be a good thing for her emotionally to separate herself mentally from Levi. After all, he would soon belong to someone else, and that person wasn't Maggie.

Oh how she wished that Levi had considered her more than just a friend. Best buddies, they were, and perhaps that would never change. All these good works and care that Levi showed her were nothing more than what best friends would do, right?

Okay. Okay. No time to think about that.

Maggie wanted to go to church this morning, but she knew that might not be the right thing to do. What if she not only had a stomach bug—like the urgent care physician said—but actually the flu or something serious? She didn't want to infect thousands of people at Midtown Chapel.

In all of Maggie's life, she hardly missed church in person except when she had been sick.

If she could make it, she would. Rain or shine, sleet or snow, flash flood or thunderstorms. None of those mattered. Unless the church was closed for a reason or she was out of town, she'd be there. In fact, if she were out of town, and couldn't find a local church to attend, she'd livestream the church service, so it was as though she was there vicariously.

Church wouldn't start until eleven o'clock. She had about twenty five minutes to brush her teeth and read her Bible. These days, she liked to read her Bible in the sunroom because there was more...sunshine. Winter moved the sun around the house, and her bedroom didn't get as much sun as this part of the house.

She sat down at her favorite desk—the one that Levi had given to her and Malachi. Her Bible and journal were exactly where she'd left them...

Oh no.

The Post-It note was still on the table.

Surely Levi had seen it when he'd come here to get her phone in the middle of the night before they left for urgent care.

She cringed. Why had she written that note-to-self?

When Levi had brought her the phone, he hadn't said a thing to her. He seemed a bit concerned about the moving boxes, but he didn't press for an answer when she said she'd tell him later. He probably didn't want to be the last person to know.

Perhaps Maggie was overthinking this.

Levi might be concerned about her, but she reminded herself that they were only friends. At least, Levi had never shown that he cared for her beyond a simple friendship. No perks, no privileges. Just two Christian friends who attended the same church and worked there as well.

If not for the Midtown Village, Maggie might not have known Levi that well. If she had only worked at the women's ministry office at Midtown Chapel in downtown Atlanta, she wouldn't have spent so much time at the Midtown Village, especially in the Christmas season, and wouldn't have needed supplies from the church warehouse where Levi worked.

In the twenty-two months since Levi's breakup with Soline, Maggie had not once disclosed to Levi that she had begun to like him more than as just a friend. She was afraid Levi would run and that'd ruin their friendship.

She'd rather love him secretly and quietly in her own way. It would be best if he never knew that she'd somehow fallen in love with him.

It was her fault that she had. It was all one-sided and it couldn't last. She'd get over it once Levi started dating Forsythia as he so wanted. She'd leave town and forget about him.

Maggie washed her face and brushed her teeth. She usually read her Bible before she showered, and so she did. Being able to keep that routine meant that she was on the mend.

She thanked God as she continued reading through her Bible. She was in 1 Peter 3:8-9 today and felt that God was speaking to her.

Finally, all of you be of one mind, having compassion for one another; love as brothers, be tenderhearted, be courteous; not returning evil for evil or reviling for reviling, but on the contrary blessing, knowing that you were called to this, that you may inherit a blessing.

A blessing.

Yes, Maggie wanted to be a blessing to Levi. Perhaps that included helping Levi find a good Christian girlfriend, who could eventually become his wife.

As long as Levi was in God's perfect will, Maggie would be happy to let him go. Levi might not be for her after all.

Most importantly, Maggie wanted God's best for Levi.

Maggie prayed for God's will to be done in Levi's life and also in her life and her new job in Florida. At this moment, she felt that she was doing the right thing leaving Atlanta. That way, she wouldn't interfere in Levi's life.

He seemed sure that he was meant to have Forsythia, even though at this point, she was still ignoring him. The ice-breaker had come Saturday night and Maggie had ruined it by falling sick and getting Levi all concerned for her.

"I'll make up for it." Maggie reminded herself to text Alden sometime today to remind him that they were setting up a blind date for Forsythia. "That needs to be soon, maybe in the next few days."

She made her way back to the living room, happy that her stomach ache was subsiding. She was grateful that Levi had insisted on taking her to urgent care, and thankful to God that the clinic was open at all on a Sunday morning.

Sitting on the couch with the Bible on her lap, Maggie accessed the Midtown Chapel website where the livestream was happening. She could have connected the laptop to the big screen television via an HDMI cable, but she didn't feel up to it.

The church service started with on-screen announcements and reminders to tithe and sign up for believer's baptism. As usual, Mrs. Smith was at the piano, playing a medley as people took their seats.

The giant screens on two ends of the stage displayed announcements.

"Don't miss the Christmas play this weekend. Three evenings only. Invite your friends. Friday night is sold out, but Sunday matinee tickets are still available. Skip your nap, bring a neighbor. Find these announcements and more on your church app and website. Sign up for them at either place. Or scan the QR code on this screen."

The music director and his worship ensemble took the stage.

Ping!

Maggie picked up her phone from the coffee table. It was a message from Levi. She had forgotten to text him when she woke up. Well, did that mean she was really letting him go—since she hadn't thought of him since he dropped her off this morning?

> MAGGIE
>
> I'm awake and fine. Thank you for taking me to urgent care. I'm livestreaming the service on my laptop. Maybe I'll see you in the audience.

> LEVI
>
> You need proof that I'm in church?

> MAGGIE
>
> Haha.

> LEVI
>
> Thank God you're getting better. I prayed for you this morning. I went home to change. I didn't make it to Sunday school but I'm in church now and will take notes for you.

> MAGGIE
>
> Okay.

> LEVI
>
> I'll come over after church and cook chicken soup for you. I'll bring lunch. What do you want for lunch?

> MAGGIE
>
> Again, you don't have to.

LEVI

I want to. Want me to surprise you for lunch? Then you can tell me how well I know you.

MAGGIE

Whatever.

LEVI

If you need anything else at the grocery store, text me before noon.

MAGGIE

Okay. Thanks, Levi.

LEVI

Back to church. See you at lunch.

Maggie wondered what the surprise would be. How well did Levi know her? How well did Levi think he knew her?

Yes, it did feel that what they had was a simple friendship between two Christians. Nothing more, nothing less. That fact was solidified when Levi asked her to help him get a date with Forsythia.

Speaking of whom, Maggie hadn't completed her task for Levi yet. It was going to happen. Alden was helping her to get ahold of Forsythia. Once she and Levi went out to dinner, Maggie's job was done.

She could finally retire from being Levi's matchmaker.

After singing hymns—old and new—with the congregation, Maggie checked her church app on her phone to see which passage of the Bible she should put her bookmark on.

As soon as she saw the verse, she drew a deep breath. Proverbs 16:9. Dad had preached on this verse before, and so had Malachi. In fact, it had been Malachi's first sermon right out of seminary.

> *A man's heart plans his way,*
> *But the Lord directs his steps.*

On screen, Pastor Kim looked formal in his suit, his usual attire in the second service at church. In the first service the seventy-year-old pastor was usually more relaxed, not wearing a coat and tie. In the next service, he'd wear his usual formal attire.

Sometimes she wondered if Pastor Kim used the early service to warm up for the second service, but she had attended both services back to back before, and he preached the same way both times.

Suit and tie were Pastor Kim's staple, reminding Maggie of the church history. Midtown Chapel had kept its tradition from a hundred years ago when people dressed in their Sunday best to church. No beach flip-flops and bikinis in the sanctuary for church members, but that didn't apply to visitors. If one should walk in from the neighboring hotel pool dressed as such, the church wouldn't turn the soul away.

Atlanta was a tourist town, and in any given year, there would be millions of visitors coming and going, especially now that the entire state of Georgia was open as film sites. Many award-winning movies had been made in the state. That not only meant that cast and crew came and went through Georgia, but also tourists who wanted to see film sites and fictitious towns with their own eyes.

Given the change toward a more casual atmosphere on weekends, most churchgoers at Midtown wore casual attire. A Hawaiian shirt here, and a pair of jeans there. That made it less off-putting for visitors and tourists who dropped in on Sunday mornings if they were walking about downtown and saw this historic church at the corner of Spring Street, blocks away from the Fox Theatre.

Yeah, it would feel like downtown to tourists who didn't know the city, but Midtown Chapel was technically located in the midtown area, away from the Atlanta city center. Traffic there was just as bad, but Maggie felt at home with an urban lifestyle.

Atlanta was her hometown. She and Malachi might be two of the rare Georgia residents who had been born in Atlanta. There were many transplants in the city and transient residents as well. At least half of her friends were from out of town.

Even Levi had been born in Savannah. Speaking of which, Maggie wondered if Levi was planning to spend Christmas in Savannah, as he had done for many years.

"Let's pray." Pastor Kim's voice popping out of the laptop speakers reminded Maggie to focus.

She closed her eyes and asked God to forgive her mind for wandering.

Chapter Eight

$\mathcal{M}$aggie woke up to the smell of chicken soup and the noise of pots and pans in the old kitchen. She opened her eyes groggily, turned—

And rolled off the edge.

Her body landed on a rug, and her ankle hit something hard. "Owww!"

She opened her eyes. Wrapped in a blanket, she was on the floor rug in between the couch and the coffee table. She had lost a sock, but the flannel pajama pants covered most of her legs.

Something metallic dropped in the kitchen, and Maggie heard footsteps running across the oak floor toward her.

"Are you okay?" Levi's voice.

Levi and her brother were the only two single

men in her life who were allowed to come and go in her house. They both had their own set of keys to the Jacobs family home.

However, right now, Maggie wished Levi wasn't there.

How embarrassing it was for her to fall off the couch!

She tried to get up. Levi extended two arms to her and pulled her up. She sat back down on the couch, blanket still wrapped around her.

"What time is it?" She rubbed her ankle.

"Three o'clock."

"What?"

"Your lunch is in the fridge. I ate mine because I was famished."

Maggie closed her eyes and drew a deep breath. Okay, she was watching the sermon online. She stayed awake through the entire sermon about seeking God's will—Pastor Kim seemed determined to finish that series before he preached about Christmas—but she must have fallen asleep at the closing prayer.

And slept for a good three hours.

"Are you hungry? Want your lunch now?" Levi asked. "Chicken soup won't be ready until dinner."

Maggie felt a little hungry. "Yeah. What did you buy for me? I can eat something."

She tried to get the blanket off but it went around her. She got up and unwrapped the blanket. "I'm going to wash my face."

Levi nodded as Maggie made her way to her bedroom and the bathroom inside.

She had brushed her teeth this morning, but for good measure, she brushed her teeth again. After her face felt clean and smelled of fresh soap, she returned to the living room.

Levi was wearing Malachi's apron and washing dishes in the old farmhouse sink. So domestic.

Behind him, something was bubbling in the stock pot on the stove.

"Did you bring the stock pot?" Maggie didn't have one.

Levi nodded. "I'll have to take it home with me. Your dishwasher is too low for the big pot."

"You're the only one I know who takes hours to cook chicken soup." Maggie stopped at her parents' avocado green vintage refrigerator.

"Only the best for you, Mags. Family recipe from Aunt Marie."

"You better not let your future girlfriend hear that."

"What do you mean?"

"She's the only one who should get your best, Levi. Not me."

Levi seemed amused, like he wasn't sure if he agreed with Maggie. He'd have to learn it the hard way. Maggie wasn't sure if he got the message she was trying to convey.

Levi turned off the faucet and dried his hands. He opened the refrigerator to retrieve a tray of vegan sushi. "No fish in this one, okay? Just cucumbers, carrots, and avocado wrapped in rice and seaweed. Can you eat it?"

"I think so—since it's mostly rice. Thanks for getting it for me. I heard that rice can help my tummy at this time."

"BRAT diet. Bread, rice, applesauce, and toast." Levi set it on the peninsula that connected to the kitchen sink. It was low enough for people to sit around, and Maggie's family had called it the breakfast counter.

"Do you want this on a plate?" Levi asked.

"No. I'll eat it off the tray." Maggie washed her hands again, even though she'd just done that in the bathroom.

"I ate as soon as I arrived. You were sleeping and I didn't want to wake you up." Levi handed her a fork. "In fact, I knew I would be making a lot of noise in the kitchen. I wanted to put you in the bedroom, but didn't want to drop you on the way there since I haven't been to the gym in a few years."

"Are you saying I'm too heavy for you to carry?" Maggie raised her eyebrows.

"No."

"If you can't carry me, how can you carry your bride across the threshold in the future?" Maggie walked around the breakfast counter to sit down on the other side, facing Levi in the kitchen.

"Do they still do that nowadays?" Levi asked.

"I have no idea. My attendance at weddings usually ends at the reception."

"Mine too."

Maggie sat down on a chair and said grace quietly, thanking God for the sushi lunch. "How much is this, Levi? I'll reimburse you."

"No need. In return for lunch and dinner, you can tell me what exactly is going on, Mags."

"What do you mean?"

"Don't leave out the details. I can take it. Tell me why you quit your job at Midtown Chapel so abruptly that even I didn't see it coming. Did you get into an argument with someone? Did you get bullied at work? Did Mrs. Kim fire you?"

Maggie laughed. "You have some imagination. The answers are: no, no, and no. I left after much prayer."

"You often tell me your prayers."

"Not all."

Levi seemed to think there was more. Well,

Maggie wasn't going to tell him. Not now, and maybe not ever.

"Don't make me call Tally." Levi dropped a name he shouldn't have.

Tally Fitzpatrick, whom Maggie used to work for at church, was now a friend and confidante. Mrs. Kim said she would love to have Tally make the keynote speech at the next women's conference at Midtown, but the honors of inviting her would no longer be Maggie's.

Yes, Levi knew that Maggie sometimes asked Tally for life advice. Even though Tally now lived in the Bahamas, they were still in the same time zone.

"Why did you mention Tally?" Maggie asked.

"I know you have a cover story that you tell people at church, but if I want to know the truth about your situation, only you alone can tell me. But failing you, I could call Tally. She's a friend of mine too."

"Tally won't tell you, so don't bother. That would be like me asking your cousin to spill the tea." Maggie smeared wasabi on the little rolls of sushi. "I will tell you what you need to know. The rest, just don't ask."

"I should have said I'll call your brother. I'm sure Malachi will talk to me." Levi loaded the dishwasher.

Maggie shrugged. "Malachi does what Malachi does."

"I know that there's something more to this move," Levi said. "If you were moving out of your parents' house to your own place, you would have told me. I didn't know until last night that you were packing up."

"You're not family, so why should I tell you?"

"May I remind you that we're besties?"

"May I remind you that once you have a girl-friend, this buddy system between you and me has to end."

"You keep saying that but my first date night with Forsythia isn't until Tuesday."

Ah, Tuesday. So the date is set.

"Did Alden call you or something?" Maggie kept eating.

"We ran into each other after church this morning." Levi closed the dishwasher door. "Said it would've been a double date, but the reservation was only for two."

"It's fine. It would be best to just leave you and Forsythia alone. We don't need to chaperon you. You're adults."

"I see." Levi frowned.

"You see what?"

"You were supposed to have dinner with him. What an opportunist." Levi leaned down at the table and his eyes met Maggie's. "Were you thinking he's a prospect?"

"Why are you like that? Why can't I go out with Alden? What is it to you who I go out with?"

"Snappy, are we?"

"Look. Why is it okay for you to go out with Forsythia, but not okay for me to have dinner with Alden?" It seemed that Levi was crossing the line and interfering with her love life. Was he still a best friend?

"Alden's not your Mr. Right." Levi looked like he wanted to say more, but didn't.

"And who might that be?" Maggie looked up, directly into Levi's eyes.

She couldn't say the world stood still for a brief moment because it didn't. In fact, she felt awkward.

He stepped back. "I'm your best friend and I'm only looking out for your best interest, Mags."

Levi went back to the stove to check on his simmering chicken. He turned the stove down.

"Maybe I don't want you to be my best friend anymore."

"Is that why you're leaving me?" He pointed to the boxes all around them.

It was time to talk about the boxes. "My parents are in their seventies. I've only seen them once a year after college. I thought they'd retire in

Atlanta, come back to this old house, and stay with me. However, that's not the case. They want to retire where the weather is warmer all year round."

Levi stared at Maggie. "That's it?"

All you need to know, Levi. "Mrs. Kim will make the announcement to the staff about my departure when they start posting the job opening."

"You can't be replaced, Mags." Levi leaned against a kitchen counter that was older than both of them, his arms folded. "Already it takes a full-timer to handle half your job at the Village. Erika told me she couldn't believe you did all that work plus your work as ministry assistant at church."

"I'm single, live alone, have no hobbies."

"Your hobby has been to take care of me." Levi came around and sat down in a chair next to Maggie.

"You're such a joker, Levi."

"Obviously you need a joke or two. You seem sad to leave town, and I recall you loved your job. It was the only thing you ever wanted to do, you said. And now you've quit. Something doesn't add up."

He leaned toward her. His bright brown eyes stared at her under the ceiling light.

Every time he sat closer to her, she felt her hands sweating and her heart thumping hard. It had been like that since Levi came to her after Soline left him. At first they were friends talking about life in general. Then they were talking about their own lives.

And Maggie fell in love.

It had to stop somewhere since it seemed to be a dead end with Levi. She felt that leaving Atlanta was the best thing she could do to regain her sanity.

One-sided love could never go anywhere. It felt like a cruel joke.

The last time she had chatted with Tally, Tally asked if Maggie saw it as a love triangle between her and Levi and Forsythia. Technically, it wasn't because Maggie wasn't pursuing Levi at all. She simply sat there with her secret love and a broken heart, waiting for Levi to notice her. At the same time, Levi would have dated someone else had it not been Forsythia. The fact that Levi, the supposedly shining knight, couldn't get an audience with Forsythia, the queen, was what had made Levi press the issue. Had to get face time with the queen!

However, Maggie—and now Alden—were going to help him. Was it good or bad? Maggie couldn't tell in the midst of the fog in her own heart.

Still, if Levi wanted to date Forsythia, Maggie

would do everything she could to help him. As long as he was happy, then Maggie could be happy. She felt like Cyrano de Bergerac in that play she watched in college. Cyrano and his friend loved the same woman, and Cyrano did everything he could to help his friend get the woman, at his own expense.

What if whom Levi wanted wasn't whom God wanted for him? Then that would be Levi's own problem.

Maggie dared not pray for an alternative outcome. She could only pray for God's perfect will to prevail in Levi's life.

And mine too.

"Are you running away from something?" Levi finally asked. "Someone?"

"Am I?"

"Are you running away from me, perhaps?"

That came out of the blue. What was he thinking?

"Why would you say that?" Why would Levi think that she was running away from him? Had he sensed anything?

Tell him already.

Tally's words came to her mind. In a way, Tally was right. Maybe Levi should choose between Maggie and Forsythia.

No. Forsythia was this amazing award-winning

chef de cuisine. Camera-ready pretty to boot, with a lovely tall figure. She should've been on television with Chef Stephanos, someone Forsythia admired.

Chef Stephanos, formerly of St. Augustine, Florida, had moved to Atlanta to host a cooking show in which he met with local Southern chefs to cook with them. In the metro city, he moved around in RYUCP circles, hosting charitable events for the architecture company.

That had been how Alden, the ministry assistant to the top brass at RYUCP, met Chef Stephanos.

And it was enough to make the blind date on Tuesday happen. It was a blind date to Forsythia, but Levi knew he was having dinner with her.

The only thing Maggie did was talk to Alden on Saturday morning about Forsythia. Maggie had no idea what ropes Alden had pulled to get someone to give up their dinner reservation on Tuesday night so that Forsythia and Levi could get to know each other. Unfortunately, it was a table for two, not four.

Alden suggested that he and Maggie go elsewhere, but she turned him down.

She had succeeded in getting Levi a date with Forsythia. But she felt numb. In a way she was happy that Levi got what he wanted, but she was sad that it was at her own expense.

Levi looked like he wanted to say something else, but Maggie had already forgotten her question or what they were talking about. She finished the last roll of sushi.

Her phone rang, as if on cue.

Forsythia.

"I'll take care of this." Levi started to clean up the counter.

Maggie took her phone and walked away. "Hi Forsythia. What's up?"

She walked through the maze of boxes to the closed-off sunroom that was now an extra sitting room with a couch that doubled as a pull-out bed. She sat on the couch and looked outside. Trees with bare branches scattered across the yard, and among the trunks, she spotted Levi's pickup truck parked in the driveway on the other side of the small grove.

"Do you know who I'm having dinner with on Tuesday night?" Forsythia got down to business.

"Yes, I do."

"But you can't tell me."

"No."

"Per Alden, isn't it?"

"It's a part of our arrangement."

Forsythia sighed. "Last time he hid something from me, it ended up being a prank."

"What was the prank?"

"That I would be invited to a cooking show. It didn't happen. It was April Fool's Day. I didn't know it was already April then."

"Was this back in Savannah?"

"Yeah. Alden was trying to cheer me up because I had a hard time. That's what friends are for, he said."

Friends. Here we go again.

Maggie wanted to rethink all this friendship thing. Why couldn't she just tell Levi that she loved him? Then again, if he rejected her, wouldn't she feel embarrassed?

So now she was running away. Levi had been right.

"If not for Chef Stephanos, I wouldn't have agreed to the blind date," Forsythia said.

"What exactly did Alden tell you?"

"That it takes a month to get a dinner reservation, and his architect friend gave it up so that I could have this blind date. How could I turn down eating at Stephanos for free?"

Free.

That meant Levi was going to pay a pretty penny for dinner where it would cost an upward of a hundred dollars per person—and more if they drank alcohol.

Thankfully, Levi didn't.

Maggie didn't know if Forsythia was a drinker, since they had only known each other as coworkers and they had never met after hours.

"Alden also said there is a possibility that Chef Stephanos might stop at our table. I would love to meet him. I'm going to bring two cookbooks for him to sign."

"You're going to bring cookbooks to your blind date?" Maggie wondered what Levi would think if he knew that Chef Stephanos was more important to Forsythia than Levi.

"Tell me about my blind date." Forsythia sounded excited. "Don't tell me his name. See if I can guess."

"Oh?"

"If he can afford dinner at Stephanos, then…"

Then what, exactly? Maggie didn't pursue it. "What do you want to know?"

"Alden said you know him well."

"Perhaps. Ask away." Maggie leaned back on the couch. The afternoon sun shone in on her pajamas. That was when she realized she was wearing pajamas in the afternoon with Levi in the house.

Then again, Levi didn't care what she wore in

front of him. On the other hand, Maggie tried to keep it modest.

"I'll ask you random questions," Forsythia said. "What's his favorite color?"

"Blue." Maggie didn't have to think at all to answer this one.

"Favorite time of day?"

"Dusk."

"Christian song?"

"I think he likes 'Resurrecting' by Elevation Worship."

"I like that too. How about his favorite Christmas carol?"

"Maybe both 'O Holy Night' and 'O Come, O Come, Emmanuel.' But he also likes other Christmas songs. He has a playlist."

"Wow. Seems like you know him well."

"I do. Any other favorites you want to know?"

"Season?"

"Winter. He doesn't like summer because it's too hot." Sadly, summer all year was where Maggie was headed.

"How many siblings does he have?"

"He's an only child." Maggie didn't want to go into details, but she added, "His parents are deceased. He was raised by his aunt and uncle— both of whom are also now deceased, sadly."

Maggie wondered if giving out that sort of

information would work against her own personal interest. Then again, the more Forsythia knew about Levi, the better she would treat him, right?

A tear rolled down Maggie's face. She wiped it with the back of her hand.

Another tear rolled.

"What's his favorite food?" Forsythia asked, oblivious to the plight Maggie was in on the other end of the phone.

"Seafood gumbo." Maggie cleared her throat.

Another tear fell.

"Fruit?"

"Kiwi."

"One last question. His favorite vacation place?"

"At home…" Maggie closed her eyes as more tears covered her cheeks. Why was she so emotional today?

She felt bad. She should be happy for Levi.

She felt a tissue on her eyes and cheek. *Dab. Dab.*

She opened her eyes.

It was Levi. He handed her a wad of tissues, now moistened with her tears. And took the phone out of her hand. He hung up the phone without a goodbye.

"No need to torture yourself, Mags." Levi sat down next to her.

This was the second time this afternoon that Levi had sat down next to her on a couch.

His arms went around Maggie. Maggie resisted. Pushed him back. Her heart could not take it.

"Just let me hold you," Levi said softly.

Maggie hesitated.

"I'm your best friend—meaning, I'm also your closest friend."

"Are you?"

He nodded, arms open wide.

And Maggie cried on his chest.

Chapter Nine

Stephanos had an understated decor and sleek lines, minimalistic architecture that made Levi feel cold and insipid. He had to wear a jacket to eat here—a jacket that Maggie had helped him to select—and he felt constricted. He'd rather wear a tee shirt and eat a hamburger with Maggie somewhere else.

Clearly it had been a mistake to pursue Forsythia all these months, only to realize in his heart on Sunday afternoon that she wasn't the one. Still, he had to go through with the dinner plans.

This Tuesday evening, at this expensive place that could put him out by a few hundred dollars—including tips—Levi would say goodbye to his short-lived crush. It all felt silly to him now as he was about to lose someone dear and close to him, someone he should have loved instead of looking elsewhere.

He had broken Maggie's heart, and he was here tonight, on a date with Forsythia, to end his rabbit trail.

They had driven separately as Levi had requested. He planned to leave early. If only he could have canceled this dinner, but it was too late. Might as well show up, even though this was probably the last time he would step into such an establishment as he surely couldn't bring Maggie to a place with this evening's memory.

Forsythia appeared with the maître d'.

She looked lovely in a simple red dress. Her five-inch heels were studded with rhinestones—or real diamonds, perhaps. She wore her hair up, and there was a pretty gold necklace around her neck.

She placed two hardcover cookbooks on the table before the maître d' seated her and placed the cloth napkin on her lap.

"Please tell Chef Stephanos that Chef Forsythia is here." Forsythia's voice was calm, but her eyes were all excited.

"Yes, ma'am." The man nodded and left.

Levi realized now that Forsythia hadn't spoken to him yet. The cookbooks told Levi all he needed to know about why Forsythia agreed to dinner with him tonight.

"I suspected it was you." Forsythia smiled. It seemed like a genuine smile.

"Me?"

"When Maggie answered my questions on Sunday afternoon, she gave me the impression that she knew you very well. Like really well. There was no hesitation in her answers."

"I heard Maggie sob on the phone, and then she hung up on me because she could barely speak."

Well, the last part of it wasn't exactly true. Levi didn't want to tell Forsythia that he had been the one who hung up the phone. It was none of her business that he had spent a lot of time with Maggie—both at work and outside of work.

"Maggie and I are coworkers at church, and I also consider her a friend. I don't want to hurt her feelings—especially at Christmas, of all times. Clearly she cares about you." Forsythia looked around, as if Chef Stephanos would appear any minute now.

"She wants the best for me. Don't blame her. I asked her to help me with this dinner, and somehow Alden got involved. I'm glad he did because otherwise we wouldn't be having a conversation as we just did in this fancy place."

"I've seen you both together at church and at Midtown Village all year. I thought you were an item." Forsythia sighed. "Come to find out you were only friends. That's a shame. If I were that close to a guy, we'd be dating almost right away."

"Maggie is my best friend. I try to keep my love life separate from my counselors."

"I disagree with that mentality." Forsythia pointed red manicured nails at him. "My parents met in chef school and married each other after only a few weeks of dating. They're celebrating their fiftieth wedding anniversary in April."

"Congratulations."

"Dad said that his best friend is Mom and only her. He said that he would rather not have married anyone at all if he couldn't be best friends with his wife."

"Oh."

"They do everything together, read each other's minds, laugh at each other's silly jokes." Forsythia's eyes were far away. "When you know someone that well, it's so much easier to be on the same page in a marriage and talk about deep spiritual things with her. Right?"

Was Forsythia teaching him a lesson? Levi wasn't sure he wanted to hear any of these things.

"Thing is—if your BFF is outside your marriage and is of the opposite gender, what would your future wife think?" Forsythia asked. "Does the marriage vow that says 'forsaking all others' mean anything to you?"

"I haven't thought that far."

"You might not have, but some of us women do. If I know Maggie well enough, she would have thought about it. How could she be your best friend when you're married to someone else?"

Levi had to admit that Maggie had mentioned something similar more than once.

"Someone else should be sitting in this seat instead of me."

Levi said nothing.

"Do you always want your relationship with Maggie to be platonic?"

"I have no idea."

"Then let me ask you this. What if she marries someone else—like Alden—and then she can't be your best friend anymore?"

Alden? Not him.

Levi felt his blood boil. Like he had to leave right now and go rescue Maggie.

Forsythia tapped the table with her fingernails. "You want Maggie, don't you? More than her friendship, you want her to stay with you for maybe the rest of your life. You don't want to share her emotions with Alden."

"What are you talking about?" Levi felt

lectured on, and yet he felt somewhat relieved that some restraints were being removed from him.

Perhaps Forsythia was here to tell him something that no other woman he knew could. Maggie wouldn't because she didn't have this personality. Her empathy for Levi was too strong. He couldn't ask his cousin's wife, Amy, because she didn't know Maggie.

Here was Forsythia, who had nothing to lose, giving him wise counsel out of the blue—although this session would cost him the price of dinner for two.

"What am I talking about? Do you know why Alden went to all this trouble to make this dinner happen?"

"Tell me." Levi sipped some sparkling water from the blue goblet. He realized they hadn't ordered yet, but he wanted to know what Forsythia had to say about Alden.

"Because if you and I date, then Alden is free to date Maggie."

Levi nearly dropped the goblet. He told himself to remain calm. So Alden had an ulterior motive.

"See, am I right or am I right?" Forsythia chuckled. "I think you and Maggie are already more than friends."

"What do you mean?"

"Who do you go to when you have a bad day?"

Maggie, of course. But Levi didn't answer. Maybe people had seen him drop by Maggie's office often, drinking the coffee she made, and sitting on the couch watching her work.

"Who do you tell secrets to that you tell no one else?"

Maggie.

As far as Levi knew, no one had seen him go to her house, complaining about the lack of love in his life. At the start of the year, Malachi had been there in the same house for a few months, so Levi didn't think it was a big deal to show up uninvited to pal around with his buddies.

After Malachi accepted the assistant pastor position at Lakeside Chapel, he left Atlanta. Levi continued to visit Maggie in that old house with its old furnishings—because they were buddies. Malachi seemed to approve of it because he didn't say otherwise.

Perhaps he should stop going to see Maggie.

Three more weeks and he wouldn't be seeing her as much anymore.

For some reason, Levi felt sad thinking about that.

"I'm glad you're finally getting the memo. So what are we doing here tonight?" Forsythia asked.

"Maybe you can get your cookbooks signed. I'll pay for our dinner as an apology for taking time out of your busy December."

"It will be worth it just to speak with Chef Stephanos."

"Then let that be our goal tonight. Nothing more."

"Deal." Forsythia studied the menu. "They changed it. I suppose this is their winter rotation. I'm not sure I like anything…"

"Nothing at all?" A male voice spoke.

Levi looked up.

The chef de cuisine was here.

He was tall and looked younger in real life than his photos on Instagram. He seemed to be in his mid thirties. Levi had to admit that he hadn't watched any of Chef Stephanos's television shows, but Maggie had shown him some clips on YouTube.

Forsythia stumbled in her words and turned beet red. She almost stood up.

"No, no. No need to stand up for me, Chef Forsythia. I'm here to receive critique from you that I didn't get with my Michelin star."

Oops. Poor Forsythia.

Levi didn't know what to say to help her.

"How did you know my name?" Forsythia looked surprised.

"Your name was on the reservation. You told the maître d' to let me know when you arrived. And I have your photo from a friend of a friend of a friend."

"At RYUCP."

Chef Stephanos nodded.

Forsythia smiled, as if she appreciated being acknowledged by a celebrity chef. "I must defend myself, Chef Stephanos. I merely said that I wasn't sure about your menu. I didn't say I was certain I didn't like this or that. Besides, I was only on the front page of your menu."

"There is no back page."

"No?" Forsythia flipped the menu over. "Oh."

"Chef Forsythia, if you think my menu is lacking, I invite you to come to my kitchen and taste the dishes."

Forsythia almost got up. Her eyes widened. "Right now?"

"I suppose it's all right if it's fine with your date."

Levi raised a hand. "We're not dating. We're just colleagues at work, here to have you sign her cookbooks."

He was sure of what he spoke. He felt a calmness in his heart, now that he knew that letting Forsythia go was the right thing to do.

As for Maggie, he wasn't sure where that relationship would lead. He knew he had to decide soon because Maggie would be moving away in three weeks.

Or perhaps he didn't have to decide now. He could let it flow where it might. That would give him time to pray about it and seek God's will.

Why hadn't he thought of that when it came to pursuing Forsythia?

Forsythia got out of her chair and chatted with Chef Stephanos.

"Don't forget your cookbooks," Levi said to her.

"Yes." Forsythia picked up the cookbooks.

"I have to leave shortly, but perhaps you two can sit at this table," Levi suggested. "Unless the Chef is working tonight."

"Are you giving up your seat?" Chef Stephanos asked.

"I'll still pay for dinner if you wish."

"No, dinner is on the house because Chef Forsythia has challenged my menu."

"Well, let me stay out of the drama then." Levi put his napkin on the table. "I best be going. Someone needs me at home—I mean, at her home."

"Say hi to her for me, will you?" Forsythia's voice wasn't bitter at all. Her focus seemed to be elsewhere.

Levi nodded.

After wishing the two chefs a good evening, Levi left the restaurant. He threw his jacket in the backseat of his pickup truck, and started the engine. But he didn't leave the parking lot.

"Lord, I have a lot to learn. I'm sorry I'm such a late bloomer at thirty-three years old. What now?"

Forsythia had implied that Maggie had feelings for him. Did he have feelings for Maggie?

But first things first. He knew he had to ask Maggie to forgive him for using her to get a date with Forsythia. At the same time, it seemed that he had watched Romans 8:28 play out at the restaurant.

And we know that all things work together for good to those who love God, to those who are the called according to His purpose.

Even his non-date dinner with Forsythia had yielded insight into a matter that Levi hadn't considered. Looking back, he could see that his heart was bent toward Maggie.

For example, he didn't like seeing Alden helping Maggie decorate the community center at the Village.

Was that jealousy?

Yes? No? I don't know.

When Maggie moved to Florida, she'd be away from Alden. But in Florida, she might meet someone else. Would Levi be okay with that?

Uh...

He texted his cousin, Cyrus, in Savannah, to see if he had a free minute. It was a little after eight o'clock in the evening, and Levi guessed correctly that Cyrus was still awake and probably working in his home office.

Cyrus called him back on video. He was in his office, as Levi had expected. "You have a question for me because I'm married? What sort of question?"

"Maggie and me. Our friendship." Levi had chatted with Cyrus enough times this year after his breakup with Soline that Cyrus knew about Maggie.

"Friendship?"

"Maggie is leaving me," Levi said.

"Interesting choice of words, considering you're not together."

"I mean she's moving away to Florida to be closer to her parents and only brother."

"Okay."

"In Florida, she might find someone. Should I be okay with that?"

"Are you asking me that question because you have a mind fog?" Cyrus leaned into his phone.

"She and I are best friends. She was okay with me pursuing my erstwhile dream date. Therefore it follows that I should also feel fine for her to move on with her life, find a boyfriend, marry a husband, have kids."

"Is that a statement or a question, Cousin?"

"That's the problem. I'm not okay with all of the above."

"You can't do that, Levi. It's not fair to Maggie."

"I want her to be with me and only me."

"Oh." Cyrus drank from a mug. There was a tea tag hanging off the side of the mug. "Let me ask you this. How did your date night go?"

Levi shook his head. "It was a mistake, and yet it wasn't. A mistake because I focused all my attention on the wrong person. Not a mistake because tonight I learned that maybe I've moved beyond friends with Mags."

"Didn't you see this or were you in denial about her?"

"I don't know. That's why I'm asking you."

"So tonight you received advice from your non-date and now you're asking me for advice."

Levi nodded. "Before I called you, I prayed to God."

"That's what I was getting at. Let me suggest that before you ask anyone else for suggestions and solutions, that you spend time in God's Word. Your Heavenly Father sees all that's going on between you and Maggie—if there's anything at all."

Levi drew a deep breath. Cyrus was right.

Forgive me, Lord.

"At my church service on Sunday, Pastor Flores spoke about Jeremiah 33:3," Cyrus said.

Levi knew the verse by heart.

Call to Me, and I will answer you, and show you great and mighty things, which you do not know.

"We have both talked about this verse before, haven't we?" Cyrus asked.

"Yes. In the matters of work and career, we have."

"Now in the matters of the heart, I remind myself to recognize that God can show me things I do not know, like how to deal with my lovely wife and our kids."

"I need to know 'great and mighty things' about Maggie and me."

"Call to God, spend time in His Word, and let Him show you what you don't know about your relationship or non-relationship with Maggie."

"Thanks, Cy. What I needed to hear."

"You've talked about Maggie this year more than you ever talked about Soline. Did you realize that?"

"Really?"

"Why didn't you just date Maggie?" Cyrus asked.

"Because she knows too much about me. How could she…" Levi didn't know how to finish his sentence.

"Love you?"

"I don't know, Cy."

"It's called unconditional love. After knowing you all your life—since you're younger than I am —I still love you. So why not Maggie? She knows you the best—more than I know you."

Levi wondered if Maggie truly loved him. "I don't think she wants me. If she did, why did she help me get a date with Forsythia?"

"Because you're stubborn and have to learn things the hard way?" Cyrus laughed. "No, seriously, you asked her, didn't you? You said it would make you happy if she got you a date with the chef."

"If she loves me, why would she let me pursue another woman?"

"Maybe it's because she thinks it's one-sided. You don't love her back. She is letting you go."

That stung. Had that been why Maggie cried so much on Sunday afternoon?

Precious Maggie, I'm so sorry.

"You told me that you wanted her to be your one true friend," Cyrus continued. "You said she has never rejected you. She lets you drop in at her house at any time. Her brother doesn't object. They treat you like family."

"Malachi said that it's good for Maggie to have someone in town she could trust because they moved to Florida and left her behind."

"You're that someone."

"Wouldn't this be a betrayal of their family's trust in me if I develop feelings for Maggie?"

"That's why you didn't. Why you friend-zoned her and she family-zoned you."

Levi had nothing to say. He felt stuck.

"I'd hate for you to miss the person right in front of you—if she's God's perfect will for you." Cyrus sipped more tea. "If not, you two will part ways when she moves away, and that's the end of it."

Levi felt his chest tighten again.

The thought of not seeing Maggie every day bothered him.

Yes, it bothered him.

He had not felt this worried when his ex-girl-friend went on vacation for three months with her friends. In fact, he had cherished the peace and quiet he had those marvelous weeks.

He hadn't felt this uncomfortable an hour ago when Forsythia had turned him down in the most oblique of ways: by talking about Maggie, their common interest.

Right now, he was truly troubled by the thought that he might have to let Maggie go.

How could he?

Chapter Ten

$\mathcal{B}$y Friday morning, Maggie was exhausted as she dragged herself to work at the women's ministry office at Midtown Chapel. She'd had only five or six hours of sleep each night this week. After working all day, she went home and packed for her impending move.

Her silver lining was Levi, who went over to her house every evening with takeout dinner and packing tape. He brought a cart as well, so they could roll the boxes to one side of the living room to get them out of the way.

They would not be packing tonight because Levi insisted that Maggie take a break before she forgot this was Christmas season altogether. Levi suggested a plan for their evening and Maggie agreed because she couldn't think of a more economical plan.

Right now, she found herself at work at eight o'clock in the morning because Mrs. Kim had called for a meeting at nine. Maggie wasn't sure what it was all about. It might have something to do with the delayed announcement of her departure from Midtown Chapel.

The only thing she knew was that she was required to work up until her last day at Midtown Chapel. The church didn't stop when someone left. They simply rotated in another worker to take the empty seat.

All Mrs. Kim told her was that the women in ministry were having a meeting. Mostly mothers at church.

For some reason, Mrs. Kim had decided not to email the staff to let them know that Maggie would be moving away in eighteen days. Just as well. After all, Maggie had specially requested that they not give her a farewell party. She wanted to focus on Christmas instead.

Well, if she really wanted to focus on Christmas, why on earth would she decide to move in December? For someone who was supposedly good at event planning, this could be an epic fail.

Maggie regretted that she let her emotions get the better of her. The thought of losing Levi to someone else had made her run away out of town.

Yes, that was the secret truth. Only Tally knew about it.

Ironically, Levi and Forsythia hadn't worked out. Levi had told her little about their conversation in the restaurant. All he primarily said was that Chef Stephanos had whisked Forsythia away, and Levi went home.

Maggie was sure there had been more to that story, but she would wait until Levi was ready to tell her.

While making coffee for the women's ministry office, Maggie received a text from her brother, who said that her bedroom was ready for her to move in.

MAGGIE

> Thank you. I won't need it until the end of December.

MALACHI

> It's ready whenever you come. By the way, Mom and Dad decided to buy the log cabin next door. It has a deck over the lake.

MAGGIE

> The lake is stocked, as I recall.

MALACHI

> Yep. Dad thinks he can fish directly from the dock.

MAGGIE

I found some of his old rods. I think I'll take them to Lakeside myself rather than let the movers do it.

MALACHI

Whatever you think is best, sis. How's Levi doing?

MAGGIE

Why are you asking about him?

MALACHI

No reason.

MAGGIE

He's been helping me pack Mom and Dad's stuff. Also he's been busy at work.

MALACHI

Busy is good. Tell him I say hello.

MAGGIE

Will do. Have to go. Must prep for a meeting in half an hour.

After she put away her phone, Maggie wondered why Malachi asked about Levi. It must have been months ago when Malachi had asked about Levi.

Mrs. Kim came in through the door, dressed in a goose down coat. "Good morning! I knew you'd be here early."

"Good morning." *Am I that predictable?*

Mrs. Kim hung up her long coat in her office. Then she went to get a cup of coffee at the coffeemaker. "You make the best coffee. But this is not why I'm going to miss you if you move to Florida."

If?

What?

"It's a quarter 'til nine. Let's go to the conference room," Mrs. Kim said. "We'll be early and impress everyone."

"Is that where the meeting is?" Maggie asked. She glanced down at her attire. It was casual Friday, and she wore a multi-colored chenille Christmas sweater and a pair of black stretch pants. Her clogs were black.

"You're fine. Friday, remember?" Mrs. Kim walked ahead of Maggie. "Lock the doors. I left my purse inside."

"Mine too." Maggie picked up her tablet computer and slid it into her crossbody purse. Then she locked up the main door to the women's ministry office.

Keeping up with Mrs. Kim required good walking shoes. If Maggie had exercised half as much as Mrs. Kim, she'd be healthier now and have more energy. Packing up the house had shown Maggie how unfit she had been.

Levi too. Both of them needed to join a gym or something—

Oh. But I'm moving.

She blinked away another tear. *What is wrong with me?*

She still couldn't bank on Levi not finding someone else to crush on, even though he seemed to be done with that. He had said that his focus now was to give Maggie the best last Christmas ever before she moved out of state for good.

A finality.

"How's your packing coming along?" Mrs. Kim asked at the elevator. She pressed the up button to go to the main floor.

The staff offices were all in the basement, but the conference room was down the hallway from the Sunday school classes. In fact, on Sunday mornings and Wednesday nights, the conference room became an additional meeting or classroom.

"Levi is helping me pack some of my parents' stuff. Forty years worth of treasures. They collected a lot of souvenirs from the mission field."

"Levi is helping you?"

Maggie nodded. "I have a small house, so the two of us are enough. Besides, Tally's grandma, who owns the Lakeside Resort, decided to donate money to pay for movers to come next week to get my parents' stuff."

"Only your parents' things?"

"Mine, I have to pay for my own move, so to save money, Levi and I are going to drive a U-Haul to Florida. He's recruiting some big guys from the Village and the warehouse to help load the truck. Actually I don't have much because this is my parents' house so all the furniture is theirs to begin with."

The elevator door opened.

Some women Maggie didn't recognize greeted Mrs. Kim. When they entered the conference room, Maggie waved to quite a few people who had spoken at previous women's conferences at the church.

Mrs. Kim found two empty seats side by side and placed her mug on one. It was Maggie's cue to take the other seat. She sat down with her tablet and waited.

On the dot, Mrs. Kim welcomed everyone. "Some of you are from out of town, so I want to introduce myself and my assistant. I'm Lydia Kim, and my husband is the senior pastor of Midtown Chapel, Pastor Eldon Kim."

Mrs. Kim had always been humble and rarely ever introduced her husband as Dr. Kim, even though he had earned a Doctor of Divinity degree. As for Mrs. Kim herself, she had a master's degree in counseling.

She pointed to Maggie. "This is my assistant, Maggie Jacobs. Many of you have seen her in the women's ministry office when you come to talk to me or pick up props or flyers, and so forth."

Maggie waved to everyone.

"Most of us here are Christian mothers, who want to come together to encourage one another," Mrs. Kim continued. "We have all read Titus 2, in which older women are to mentor younger ones."

Everyone nodded.

"That's the purpose of our meeting today, to form a new ministry under the women's ministry," Mrs. Kim said. "To be sure, our church already ministers to moms. We help new mothers, provide relief for preschool moms, and stand alongside mothers of teenagers, as well as minister to empty-nesting moms. Plus, we all know about our church widows and homebound elderly mothers. On and on."

Everyone clapped.

"So we need a name with 'mom' or 'mothers' in it, and we need to be more intentional, strategic, and practical about it." Mrs. Kim looked around the room. "Today, we're consolidating all our ministries to mothers under the banner of Midtown Moms. I know that some of our friends from overseas spell 'moms' as 'mums,' but our focus here is primarily in the local area and statewide. If this ministry takes off and expands overseas, we will call it Midtown Mothers internationally, and our church will be the case study to help other churches worldwide to minister to moms."

Maggie started to take notes, as she always had in meetings.

"Everyone here has received a personal email from me about this ministry. If you are here today, you are the charter members of this new ministry that Pastor Kim has approved and budgeted under the women's ministry beginning in January. Until the end of this fiscal year, the women's ministry will shoulder this project under its current budget —since we will not have any conferences or workshops until next fall, at least."

Conferences? Workshops? Online and offline?

Maggie nearly clapped as she listened to Mrs. Kim.

She loved scheduling women's conferences at Midtown. She loved calling speakers, organizing activities, getting all the logistics together.

She felt a surge of excitement. She could totally serve God here—at her church home where she belonged.

Right away, she wanted to be a part of this ministry, even though it was primarily for mothers. She wanted to be involved in it, to help Mrs. Kim coordinate events. She knew God had gifted her some organizational skills that she could put to good use here, serving in the house of God.

She sensed the calling of God here at Midtown Chapel, not at Lakeside Resort working as Colette Fitzpatrick's marketing assistant. She could easily use her college communications degree to serve God in either place, but she was sure that she could feel a stronger calling here.

What now?

Maggie had already quit her job as ministry assistant in the women's ministry. Mrs. Kim had approved it, even though she was taking her time to find Maggie's replacement.

While Mrs. Kim took questions about the new ministry forming, Maggie half listened and half prayed. She felt that perhaps her resignation from her church job had been premature. She had reacted to her own unrequited love in a way that affected her own calling and career.

And ministry.

Even though she could very well minister at Lakeside Chapel, a sister church of Midtown Chapel, it would be after work and on weekends. Her primary job when she moved to Lakeside, Florida, would be to cater to the customers of Lakeside Resort.

Or would she rather be in the Lord's house every day of the week?

One thing I have desired of the Lord,
  That will I seek:
  That I may dwell in the house of the Lord
  All the days of my life,
  To behold the beauty of the Lord,
  And to inquire in His temple.

Her shoulders sagged as she remembered Psalm 27:4.

I need to pray about this.

"Pastor Kim often reminds us that when we plan a project, whether big or small, we must not set everything in stone until God sets it," Mrs. Kim said. "For now, I wanted to share with you the exciting news about Midtown Moms to spark your interest. When you see other moms during the Christmas holidays, feel free to tell them about it. As for the details, we will sort it out in the new year. That's also when we will announce this new exciting journey to the whole church."

New exciting journey.

Would this change Maggie's entire career trajectory?

Would Levi be happy that she stayed in town? Or would he not care either way? After all, he had helped her pack all week, and hadn't tried to change her mind.

What about Mrs. Kim? Why did she bring Maggie to the meeting?

Mrs. Kim answered as many questions as she could until no hands went up. "Ladies, as you can see, we don't have all the answers yet. However, we will be creating roles and we would have to fill them. For example, we need an event coordinator."

Me! Me!

Maggie almost raised her hand.

But Lakeside…

"Ladies, before we go, let's have a word of prayer." Mrs. Kim turned to Maggie. "Would you pray for us that God would bless the work of our hands in this ministry?"

"Yes, ma'am." Maggie bowed her head. Took a deep breath. "Dear Heavenly Father, thank You for always showing us what matters to You—the saving of souls and discipleship of believers—and how we're to go about carrying out Your perfect will in this world You have created. We ask You now for great wisdom to do the right thing in creating this new ministry to serve Christian mothers here at church, locally, statewide, nationwide, and also internationally."

Maggie's voice cracked. "May we always be

soft and yielding to Your guidance. If You tell us to go this way, we go this way. If You tell us to go that way, we go that way. If You tell us to stop, we stop. If You tell us to step back, we step back. May our heart always be sensitive to Your leading, and not be ashamed to follow You. In the holy name of Jesus, I pray. Amen."

A choir of *amen* resounded in the conference room.

Maggie followed Mrs. Kim out of the room. She stopped to talk. She waved for Maggie to return to the office downstairs. Maggie walked down the stairs instead of taking the elevator. Walking was her way of mitigating stress, but when she arrived at her desk, she was still as confused as she was upstairs.

She texted Levi.

Pray for me. I have a huge decision to make.

Chapter Eleven

*M*aggie was praying at her desk when she heard someone walk by her. She finished her prayer and looked up. Mrs. Kim was at her desk in her office. Through the open door, she waved to Maggie.

Maggie sat down in one of the two armchairs in the office. Mrs. Kim took the seat at the edge of the loveseat closest to Maggie.

"Do you know why we spun off Midtown Village into a non-profit organization of its own and hired Bina Marley to manage it?" Mrs. Kim asked.

That was how the pastor's wife chose to start their conversation.

Usually she would ask how Maggie was doing, but not today. Maggie sensed that Mrs.

Kim felt that time was running out, so she cut to the chase.

Maggie shook her head. She was only a ministry assistant. She wasn't privy to the formation of new ministries or the disbandment of old ones in the church. All that was above her pay grade.

"Because we have already planned to expand the women's ministry into sub-ministries to cater to the needs of Christian women. For example, Midtown Moms would serve mothers. Midtown Widows would serve widows. You get the idea."

"I see." *So why tell me when I'll be gone before the new year began?*

"We split off your ministry assistant work at the Village and handed that over to Erika Song. She answers to Bina. The women's ministry has a different trajectory from now on. We are going to minister to women of all ages and situations in life, domestic and international, whether they live in tiny homes or not. That is to say, our ministry has a wider scope than Midtown Village."

Maggie knew that. "And Midtown will continue to fund the Village for now, but the new non-profit organization is planning to raise funds outside our church. Was that a strain on our church budget?"

"Yes, and also stretched you too thin."

"Me? You thought of me?"

Mrs. Kim nodded. "Unfortunately, I was unable to tell you what our future plans were in the women's ministry until they'd been approved by Pastor Kim and the deacons."

"I understand."

"When you decided to move to Florida, that made me scramble to find someone who can not only be a ministry assistant but also an event coordinator."

"Oh."

"What will your new position be at Lakeside Resort?"

Maggie was surprised that Mrs. Kim knew where she was going. She tried to think of who might have talked to Mrs. Kim.

"Don't worry. Just know that I have friends everywhere."

Riona, Pastor "Fizz" Fitzpatrick's wife, would be among her friends, Maggie ventured to guess. After all, Pastor Fizz had been a counseling pastor at Midtown Chapel for a number of years until the Lord called him to pastor Lakeside Chapel for a year while training the next "Timothy," Maggie's brother, Malachi.

"Marketing assistant to Colette Fitzpatrick, the director of Lakeside Resort," Maggie answered. "I'll be doing similar things to what I've been doing here. I schedule things for her, manage her social media, and whatever else she needs done at the office."

"However, you will not be scheduling events."

"No. They already have an event coordinator who does that."

"Here at Midtown, you were able to schedule events in the same job you had."

"I love doing that. Organizing events for the women's ministry as well as for Tally's speaking engagements have been the highlight of my job here at the church."

"I know. Not only has Tally told me about your efficiency, I've also seen it myself this year." Mrs. Kim leaned back in the loveseat. "To be honest with you, I don't see myself entering the speaking engagement circuit. I'm not like Tally. My gift is more in the area of meeting needs and filling gaps in church."

Maggie agreed. Mrs. Kim and Tally were totally different in their approach to ministry work.

"For example, our church is growing quickly," Mrs. Kim said. "Last week our preschool area was almost bursting at the seams. While the children are ministered to, how about their mothers? Tired and overworked, no pay, no salary. How can the women's ministry better meet their needs? That's what I think about all the time."

I want to help!

Maggie waited.

"At the meeting upstairs, I mentioned that we need an event coordinator. That is to say, the women's ministry needs to find two people in January: a ministry assistant to replace you, and an event coordinator to help me organize all these activities for mothers, single women, career women, widows, and so forth. We will minister to all women at our church."

"How is the event coordinator job different from what I've been doing thus far?"

"You know what a ministry assistant is supposed to do. If I need a poster or flyer, you make me a poster or flyer. If I need to make an announcement, you write me the copy. If I need a brochure done, you make it happen. If people call the office, you answer the phone. You are all-in-one."

It was by God's mercy and grace that Maggie had been able to do that, both at church and at the Village.

"When Tally was here, she was skilled at organizing events for the women's ministry. Under her, you have learned to organize and do some of the work that she did," Mrs. Kim explained. "In many ways, you have been apprenticed and now you're a journeyman event coordinator."

"I see. So you're saying that while I was being paid as a ministry assistant, I did a lot of things outside my original job position because of Tally."

"It's not Tally's fault. We didn't give her enough human resources to do the job. So the two of you were a formidable team who could get anything done, and to do them unto the Lord without extra monetary compensation. For example, how many times have you worked extra on your own after work hours and on weekends because you couldn't get everything done in forty hours a week?"

"Especially if we have events and activities everywhere. I carry my tablet around so I don't lose track of the schedules."

"If I hire a new ministry assistant, she will most likely only be the administrative assistant and nothing more. She will be paid less than you were. She will not be organizing events in lieu of a director or managing low-income housing at the Village." Mrs. Kim paused.

Maggie began to see where Mrs. Kim was heading.

"In many churches, workers wear many hats. This is a critical problem and could lead to high turnovers at any ministry. As a counselor, I can say that doing multiple jobs under one salary and working outside your skillset can burn you out. It is my hope that Midtown doesn't cause its workers to burn out."

"Are you saying that since Tally left our church, I've been holding down three people's jobs?" Maggie hadn't been aware, but here it was.

Mrs. Kim nodded. "Is that why you resigned?"

"Not really." She wondered if she could get into the details of it. They wouldn't be what Mrs. Kim might have thought. "I actually have personal reasons I am sorting through."

"You mentioned wanting to live near your retired parents."

"Yes, that too."

"Oh. Let's talk about it then, if you want. No charge." Mrs. Kim waited.

"Now?"

"Now is fine. This is important to the health of our church."

Maggie glanced at the open door. "I left my purse in an unlocked drawer out there."

"Go get your purse, lock the front door, and we can talk." Mrs. Kim sighed. "See what I mean? If we have a ministry assistant out there, then we don't have to lock the door every time we need to talk or attend a meeting. There will always be someone at the front desk."

Maggie returned as quickly as she could.

"We can leave that door open now that you've locked the front door," Mrs. Kim said. "Is this private enough for you to talk about why you're leaving Midtown Chapel?"

Maggie nodded. "Actually, I don't want to leave Midtown at all. When I handed in my resignation at the end of November, I was very reluctant to do so. I wasn't sure if I was doing the right thing, but my heart was broken and I didn't know what else to do but to go."

"Everything we discuss here is confidential." Mrs. Kim pointed to Maggie's shoes. "Feel free to kick off your shoes and relax."

Mrs. Kim slid out of her Mary Jane shoes and folded her feet under her wool skirt as she sat on the loveseat.

Maggie kept her shoes on. She related the events in the last few months, how she had been helping Levi to snag a date with Forsythia. The entire time, her heart was in agony because she had fallen in love with Levi. She decided to keep it a secret because Levi was her best friend and she didn't want to ruin the friendship.

"You've already fallen in love with him. And yet you continued to be good friends with him, right?"

"Well, yes. Good point, Mrs. Kim. I hadn't thought of that."

"My husband and I are each other's best friends."

"I've heard. Pastor Kim has talked about your family in his sermons."

"However, the feeling is mutual between my husband and me." Mrs. Kim paused. "From what you said, you don't know if Levi feels the same way about you as you do about him."

"I think he sent me mixed signals. He cared for me, sometimes more than a friend. At the same time, he asked me to help him get a date. What kind of a person is he?"

"What do you think?"

"Maybe he was confused about his feelings." Maggie shrugged. "In any case, he was besotted with Forsythia. Every time I felt that I'd lost Levi, my heart felt sad. I couldn't stop crying. I prayed about it and I thought maybe if I moved home to see my parents for a while, I could reset my emotions. So I resigned and started packing up the house because my parents want to sell it after I leave."

"If he isn't all that into you, there's no point breaking and entering."

"That's what I thought. I didn't want to have

anything to do with him anymore. I felt that my emotional health has been adversely affected."

Mrs. Kim nodded.

"Ironically, his date with Forsythia on Tuesday night didn't go well—he won't give me details—and since that time, he has stopped talking about her."

"What does he do now?"

"He's still paying the same attention to me. We text each other every day. Tonight we're going out to eat. Then we'll come back to church for the Christmas concert."

"At least he's not asking another woman to go with him to the concert."

"Right...but now I'm confused. I'm leaving at the end of the month. If he's interested in me, he'd have to tell me now or he'd have to go to Lakeside to find me—before I find someone else. I can't wait for him forever."

"I hear you say 'now' and 'can't wait.' Patience is a fruit of the Spirit, you know. Look up Galatians 5:22-23. Sometimes called 'long-suffering,' patience requires us to wait upon the Lord."

Maggie read Galatians 5:22-23 on her Bible app.

But the fruit of the Spirit is love, joy, peace, longsuffer-ing, kindness, goodness, faithfulness, gentleness, self-control. Against such there is no law.

"I think I've been impatient with Levi," Maggie said. "At the same time, I don't want to be his fallback or backup plan."

"I hear you."

"However, if I leave now, what if I miss out on the opportunity to be with Levi?"

"Now is always a good time to pray and focus on God while you wait for Him to work in Levi," Mrs. Kim said. "If your relationship is not meant to be, then you will part ways. If Levi needs a wake-up call, let God work in him. If he needs a push, God has hands. He might use you or others to give Levi a nudge, but you wait for God to tell you so. Don't jump the gun. Rein back your patience. You're not his conscience nor the Holy Spirit. Pray for God's perfect will to be done."

"So what do I do next? Do I move to Lakeside or stay in Atlanta?" Maggie wasn't sure if anyone could answer that question for her.

"What has God called you to do? Do the last thing He has called you to do until He gives you new instructions." Mrs. Kim put her shoes back on.

"I believe that the last thing God called me to

do was to work in the women's ministry. However…"

"Is that a 'but' you're tagging on to God's instruction?"

"Well… I'm not sure if being an assistant is all I'm meant to be. I had a lot of fun organizing events with Tally. Those were the old days."

"Those days are still here. We just need to get reorganized." Mrs. Kim smiled. "Interested in the event coordinator position? You can apply for it. Pastor Kim had instructed the staff to try to promote from within before hiring someone from the outside. In the long run, it's a very cost-effective hiring plan. For example, Tally trained you for five or six years, so it would be better for the church to keep your skillset."

"Wow. I'll have to pray about that." It might mean she didn't have to move out of the family home—if she could rent it from her parents.

However, it didn't change the fact that the movers would still need to drive her parents' stuff to Florida. Mom and Dad were retiring in Florida and wouldn't be returning to Atlanta.

"Check with HR about the salary and benefits," Mrs. Kim said. "It's a different position. You'll still be in our women's ministry area, but not at the front desk."

Oh, yes. That too. If the pay was more, she

could potentially buy the family house from her parents. Rent to own or something.

It was an older house, built in the nineteen-fifties, but she could renovate it and modernize the interior. Then she could remain fifteen minutes from church, and serve God in the skill area He had gifted her.

That was the one thing she knew she should have done: obey God at the last call.

It looked like she had messed that one up. She had resigned from her church job, the one she had enjoyed very much, and secured a new job in Florida. It felt like she had abandoned God's calling for her career.

What to do now?

Then again, if she had stayed in Atlanta, worked and attended the same church as Levi, her heart would continue to break. She would watch Levi date other women and perhaps marry and go on with his life.

Meanwhile, she was stuck in her present state of one-sided love.

At the same time...

Surely she was mature enough to let Levi go. After all, this new ministry work at Midtown made her all excited about serving the Lord in her own home church. If she focused on her career and calling, then she wouldn't think of Levi much, right?

Would she be able to attend the same church as Levi?

It had only been recently—after Soline had left him—that Levi had consumed Maggie's thoughts.

Prior to that, Levi and Maggie had been friends for three years.

Things didn't have to change.

In fact, things hadn't changed. Levi only considered her his bestie, and nothing more.

They hadn't dated each other or anything like that. Levi kept a distance between them, even though he had shared all his emotional angst after he broke up with Soline. They had even discussed marriage and kids, so Maggie could tell that Levi was broken.

For almost a year, Maggie had walked with Levi through his valley. Prayed with him. Took his calls twenty-four-seven. And even cooked for him, although Levi told her not to try that one again.

"Going forward, if Levi asks me to help him find a new girlfriend, should I say no?" Maggie asked.

"Sure. You don't have to do what you're not convicted by the Holy Spirit to do. You don't owe him, do you?"

"No. I was even a pro bono matchmaker." Oh, there was a more pressing need. "What about the dinner and concert tonight?"

"Maybe you could ask a few more friends to join you. Then it wouldn't be just you two alone and won't look like a date night."

You two alone.

Uh-oh.

What about the house keys that Levi kept as backups in case Maggie locked herself out? Even though Levi had shown up uninvited when she was sick the previous weekend, she had trusted him not to cross the line.

Still, should she get her keys back?

Maggie wasn't sure. She wanted to, but would that hurt Levi's feelings? After all, those keys were Malachi's, and he'd given them to Levi himself.

"Take care of my sister," Malachi had said. "You're the only one I trust in town."

Malachi trusted Levi.

Maggie sighed.

It means Levi would never cross the line that Maggie wanted him to cross.

Friend-zoned for life seemed to be her lot.

Chapter Twelve

When Levi arrived at the Italian restaurant for the group dinner, he found Maggie at a long rectangular table, surrounded by over a dozen single people from church, including Alden and the new Midtown Village employee, Erika, both of whom were in their Sunday school class.

Not only was Levi not sitting next to Maggie, he ended up at the other end of the table, where he could not hear her nor talk to her because of the cackling laughter coming from the crowd in between them.

From the distance, Levi ate his pasta plate and watched Maggie interact with her friends sitting to the left and right of her. She looked happy.

Why hadn't he paid more attention to her? He had taken her for granted all these months.

Levi had been friends with Malachi first some years ago. That had been before Levi and Maggie somehow ended up working at Midtown Chapel at the same time. When Soline broke up with Levi, he went to see Malachi, and found that Maggie was also living in the same house.

An ordained pastor and missionary, Malachi helped him through the rough patch, and Maggie prayed with him as well as tried to comfort him. After Malachi followed Pastor Fizz to Florida, Levi continued to be friends with Maggie.

He had no problem telling Maggie anything and everything he felt because she didn't judge him. She simply listened and offered suggestions, and didn't fuss when Levi refused to listen.

Somehow several months ago, Levi thought he should start dating again, and that was when Forsythia showed up on his radar.

Perhaps he had been insensitive toward Maggie, but Levi had sought her help to get closer to Forsythia and to score a dinner date with her.

Everything seemed to be working according to Levi's plan.

Until Sunday.

When Levi heard Maggie's conversation with

Forsythia, he realized that Maggie knew a lot about him personally. Normally, Levi wouldn't think much about it. After all, he'd spent almost a year with Maggie and they got to know each other pretty well.

However, that Sunday afternoon changed everything. When Maggie cried as she answered Forsythia's questions about Levi, he knew that there was something more that Maggie hadn't said to him.

Cyrus seemed to think something was going on with Maggie, and so did Forsythia. If they could see it, not being close friends to Maggie, why hadn't Levi sensed it at all?

And what am I supposed to sense?

Maggie had been there for him all year long. Maggie had helped him through his breakup. Helped him come to his senses. Even helped him get his dream date—which he realized now had been the wrong move.

Of all the people in the world, Maggie was the person Levi most enjoyed being with. This same Maggie would be moving out of state and out of reach.

Levi found himself thinking that he couldn't let her go.

Sipping water, his eyes glanced in Maggie's direction. Surprised to find Maggie looking his way. She smiled a little and her slight dimple showed under the light.

Somehow the smile had a sad note to it.

Why, Maggie? What are we missing?

Levi finished his pasta and checked his phone for the time. An hour and a half left before the Christmas concert would begin in the Midtown Chapel sanctuary. He could leave now but...

He texted Maggie. He waited for her to reach for her purse. She always answered his messages.

LEVI

Do you have a ride to the concert?

MAGGIE

Yeah. I drove myself.

LEVI

When are you leaving?

MAGGIE

Not sure. You?

LEVI

Playing it by ear.

MAGGIE

Staying for dessert?

LEVI

IDK.

MAGGIE

You don't know? You always know.

Levi grinned. No, he didn't know anything anymore. He had almost always been sure of himself, until Soline threw him a curveball. Then with Maggie and Malachi's help, he regained his bearings. Even ventured out to try to date again. That failed, but he wasn't unhappy about it. It was a good thing that it didn't work out with Forsythia.

Now, looking at Maggie, he was starting to lose his confidence again.

They had a beautiful friendship going. He wanted to preserve it.

If he told her that his heart had closed her out because he felt that she was too precious for his messy life, that would have been true, but what kind of response would Maggie have to that confession?

If she had fallen in love with him due to sheer proximity with him, she would respond positively to him trying to break out of their friend and family zones.

If she was only really a caring friend with an acute empathy in her personality, then she might retreat from him and it would ruin their friendship.

Which category was she in?

How could he find out?

If he talked to Cyrus again, his cousin would

probably say, "Go ask her already. Let the chips fall where they may."

Levi could lose a close friend or he could gain a...girlfriend?

Oh, he couldn't imagine Maggie being his girlfriend. That would be unexpected. What would Malachi say about that?

The server came to fill his glass with water and ask if he wanted dessert.

Levi decided to indulge. He knew that Maggie's favorite dessert was strawberry shortcake with two scoops of ice cream on top. Did he want the same?

In fact, he knew a lot about her. The same questions that Forsythia seemed to have asked Maggie on Sunday, Levi knew that he could answer the same for Maggie.

Maggie's favorite color? Purple.

Time of day? Dawn.

Christian song? Also "Resurrecting." She had made it her ringtone for some months before she changed it to bird songs.

Christmas carol? She liked them all, especially "Hark, the Herald Angels Sing" and "Mary, Did You Know?"

Her favorite season? Spring when the flowers bloomed.

Fruit? Apples.

And her favorite vacation place? At home, same as Levi's.

There was nobody else in the world whom Levi knew more about than Maggie. It had to be because they'd spent almost a year together at work and after work. He wouldn't be surprised if Maggie had started to develop feelings for him.

As for him, he was fighting it. The more he looked at Maggie, the more…

In love he was?

Levi wasn't entirely sure.

One thing he knew: he didn't want Alden anywhere near Maggie.

After he had placed his dessert order with the server—making sure to tell her to put the two scoops of ice cream in a separate bowl on the side—he chatted with the people to his left and right. He might forget their names next week or in the new year, but he didn't want to come across as aloof or anti-social.

Levi was used to making small talk at church with people he came across in the hallways or in the dining room. In a mega church such as Midtown Chapel, it was hard to meet and know everyone. Which made his friendship with Maggie —and her brother, for that matter—special.

As he was talking away, he noticed that Alden got up from his seat and went over to Maggie.

What does he want?

A small red box with ribbons on top appeared in Alden's hand, and Levi's heart skipped a beat.

What are you giving her?

Levi couldn't hear what Alden said to Maggie. She smiled, took the box, and placed it on the table next to her plate of dessert.

What's happening?

Levi started to text Maggie, then changed his mind. He told himself to remain calm and take a deep breath. He'd be sitting next to her at the concert—they had agreed to sit together. He'd have plenty of opportunity to ask about the box.

When Levi's strawberry shortcake came, he texted Maggie.

LEVI:

Want my ice cream? Two scoops.

Maggie looked up from her phone, and nodded to Levi. She waved for him to bring them over.

Levi walked to Maggie, carrying the ice cream bowl in a palm, and trying to look casually nonchalant. He placed it next to Maggie's plate, right next to the mysterious red box.

"Two extra scoops of ice cream altogether in the middle of winter for Lady Maggie." Levi cast a furtive glance at the red box on Maggie's table.

To Pastor Kim and Lydia.

Oh.

It didn't say whom it was from, but Levi didn't care. It was enough that the gift wasn't for Maggie per se. He was able to breathe again and his heart felt auspiciously calm.

"You know me well, Levi." Maggie clapped.

"Always."

~

aggie and Levi drove separately from the restaurant to the church, arriving at the same time, and parked near each other, but walked into different levels of the building. While Levi saved seats for them in the church sanctuary, Maggie went downstairs to put the gift box on Mrs. Kim's desk in the women's ministry office.

She had found out this evening that Alden's parents, who lived on Hilton Head Island, knew Pastor and Mrs. Kim. They called her Lydia. Actually, Mrs. Kim had told Maggie that she could call her Lydia as well, but to this day, Maggie couldn't bring herself to. Lydia Kim was the same age as her dad, and there was just no way she could call her Lydia when she reminded Maggie of her parents.

The staff offices were quiet as everyone was either at home, out of town, or upstairs in the sanctuary. Some staff members were in the choir and in the skits. Maggie had chosen not to participate in any Christmas plays and concerts because they were not her thing. She felt that she could support the ministry best by being in the cheering section.

The only lights that were on were in the hallways, but Maggie felt safe and at home here.

She had been working at church for seven years since she graduated from a Christian college with a communications degree. Her entire career had been in a church setting. Come January she would venture out into the wide world, away from this place.

Her eyes clouded over. She blinked.

I don't know if I can leave this place.

Then again, Pastor Kim had reminded the congregation often to never worship this historical building.

"Worship Christ instead. If this building burns down, does His church still thrive? Of course."

Pastor Kim's office was around the corner, occupying the biggest space just inside of the reception desk. That way, preachers and guests didn't have to walk all over the place to get to the pastor's office, and thus, the staff could focus on work instead of dealing with non-staff foot traffic.

Maggie's phone buzzed. She checked her messages. Levi had found them seats. He told her which door to enter the sanctuary.

Maggie walked up one flight of stairs to the main level of the church. She opened the doors to the roar of people talking, with live Christmas music as the backdrop. A string ensemble next to a grand piano—which they had rolled from the choir room—played a medley of Christmas music.

Maggie hummed to "In the Bleak Midwinter" and sang a stanza of "O Little Town of Bethlehem" as the musicians played.

Reaching their designated entrance, Maggie stopped in her tracks when she spotted Levi talking with…his ex-girlfriend and her new husband.

Maggie wondered if she should give them space to chat or whether she should step in to provide support for Levi. She continued walking again to see what tone of voice Levi was using and to assess his emotional state.

He seemed to be talking amicably to Soline and Gene Lee.

Levi had come a long way since he walked out of Tally's wedding reception after Gene proposed to Soline. Maggie had opinions about proposals in someone else's wedding celebration, but nobody asked her.

Maggie smiled as she approached the trio and stood next to Levi.

As if sensing her there, Levi turned. "Dropped off the present for Mrs. Kim?"

Maggie nodded. She smiled to Soline. "Merry Christmas!"

Soline stepped forward to give Maggie a hug. "Haven't seen you since our wedding. How have you been?"

"Busy as ever." What else could Maggie say? She was, in fact, busy as ever. "How's life in New York?"

"Oh, we moved to Hong Kong." Soline wove her arm around her husband's. "Gene has a new job, so we moved."

Obviously Maggie hadn't kept up with Soline's life since they moved out of town. Like the old adage said, "out of sight, out of mind."

Maggie wondered if it would be the same for her. When she left Atlanta, would she and Levi reconnect in the future? Or would their paths diverge and never reconvene?

"They're visiting Gene's family in Duluth for Christmas," Levi explained.

"Glad you could come to the concert tonight," Maggie said.

"I heard it was sold out, so credits to Gene for ordering the tickets a month ago so we could come tonight." Soline looked at Gene lovingly.

College classmates, those two. It had to be God's will for them to reconnect.

"Well, we'd better go to our seats," Levi said. "Have a good new year, you two. When is the baby coming?"

Soline's eyes brightened. "How did you guess? Am I showing already?"

Levi shrugged. "I just guessed. Congratulations to the happy parents. May God bless you both."

Maggie was glad to see that Levi seemed to have moved on from Soline. Theirs had been such a tumultuous relationship that everyone could see a mile away that it couldn't have lasted.

Perhaps life was like this, filled with obstacles to happiness.

After a few months of chasing Forsythia, Levi finally had that dinner with her, only to make it a non-starter.

What about me? Beneath her smile, Maggie wondered if she had the courage to ask Levi point blank if there was hope for them together. So far,

Levi hadn't shown any interest beyond treating her as his closest friend.

Closer than Malachi had.

So what did this make them?

In one word: nothing.

"We're seated in the balcony, so we better find the elevator." Gene slid his arm around Soline's waist.

"Bye!" Soline waved as they disappeared into the crowd of concertgoers.

Maggie followed Levi, but people got between them as the announcement came that the doors were closing in twenty minutes. Maggie stepped back to let the crowd through so they weren't bumping her left and right.

Next thing she knew, a hand grabbed hers. She looked and it was Levi's. He pulled her forward and they entered the sanctuary.

Right away, Maggie thought of two things to suggest for next year's Christmas Concert.

Firstly, they needed to go back to numbered tickets. Midtown used to do that when the outreach pastor had been in charge. Then nobody would rush and fight for seats. After Pastor Burns had left to take up a senior pastor position in Texas somewhere, attendance to Christmas events dropped and seats were not filled. Consequently they went to a first-come-first-served arrangement. This one tonight almost resulted in Maggie being stampeded in a church, no less.

Secondly, about two years ago, the church had stopped hosting their Christmas Dinner Theater when the chef de cuisine lost his wife and fell into grief and was unable to work half the time. Eventually, he chose to retire, and they hired Chef Forsythia one year later. Maggie thought she'd find some time to talk to Forsythia about reviving the Christmas Dinner Theater—if the chef would be willing to cook for five hundred people per evening. They could spread the dinner theater over three weekends as before.

What was old could be made new again.

All these thoughts floated in Maggie's mind that she forgot about Levi, still in front of her, still leading her to their seats, and still holding her hand.

This was the first time in their three years of friendship that he had held her hand.

In front of everybody at church!

Maggie pulled her hand back, but Levi gripped it more. He glanced back and gave her a slight smile.

They made their way into the middle of a row and sat down.

Maggie looked around. "These are great seats.

We can see the orchestra clearly, and the choir too. Good job, Levi."

"Glad to help." Levi looked pleased.

Under the sanctuary lights, he didn't look distressed at all.

"What a surprise to see Soline and her husband here tonight," Maggie said. "Did you know they were coming?"

"They're not on social media much, so I didn't know until Soline called out my name."

"She did?"

"Yep. In the crowd."

"You heard her voice in the crowd…"

Levi nodded, but then added, "I can also pick out your voice in a crowd."

"Really? Mine is not high pitched like Soline's."

"But I recognize your laughter." Levi lowered his voice, almost whispering in Maggie's ear. "During those dark times in my life last year, you cried with me and laughed with me. Your laughter was my medicine, Mags. Did you know that?"

Laughter. Medicine.

"Yes, I do know that verse from Proverbs 17:22," Maggie replied.

A merry heart does good, like medicine, but a broken spirit dries the bones.

"The funniest one in the family has to be Malachi. He takes after Dad. When the two get together, they make Mom and me laugh until we cry." Maggie chuckled. "Mom said not to let Malachi make speeches at my wedding because everyone would be in tears."

Oops.

"Your wedding?" Levi's eyebrows rose.

"Just a private joke between mother and daughter. Nothing to do with you."

"Nothing at all? Are you sure? Your father likes me, you know. We were in the same disaster relief team three years ago."

"They may not like you when they do a closer inspection."

"What's not to like about me?"

"I can name a few flaws."

"I can name your flaws too," Levi retorted.

Someone in the row behind them hushed him as the lights went down and the conversation was over.

Chapter Thirteen

Standing outside the front door, Levi watched the movers drive away with a huge tractor trailer filled with everything in the Jacobs' family home except for Maggie's own things.

He shivered slightly in the late morning sun, wearing only a thick flannel shirt layered with a turtleneck. His jacket was inside the house, but it had been warm indoors all morning when he helped Maggie with the movers.

His chest constricted.

He had only felt this way three times in his life: at the funerals of his mother, Aunt Marie, and Uncle Melvin.

Uncle Melvin had probably died of a broken heart because he couldn't live without Aunt Marie, who had passed away months before he had. They had been high school sweethearts and were married for seventy-six years before the Lord took them home in the same year.

Now Levi felt that pain in his chest again, a certain feeling of grief, a fear of losing something he could never regain.

Never?

The one he felt he would miss was still inside the house behind him. Quickly, he made his way back into the house, locking the front door behind him. The living room was bare saved for a sleeper armchair that turned into a single bed at night for Maggie now that even her bedroom furniture was on its way to Lakeside, Florida.

Nearby, Maggie was staring out the side window, where sunshine shone into the living room floor, covered with dust now that the old furniture pieces had been removed.

Levi went to her and stood by her. He wasn't sure what she was looking at. Outside, the trees had shed their leaves. December was as cold as it could be in Atlanta, sans snow.

He said nothing because nothing needed to be said. He knew Maggie well enough in the last three years to know that his presence was all she needed.

He made her happiest when he spent quality

time with her. They didn't have to do anything fancy. In fact, she'd rather stay at home and do hardly anything. Not even watching television. They might listen to hymns or church music, but not today.

Today it was all silence.

Christmas was precisely a week away next Saturday, but Maggie had chosen not to play any Christmas music this morning.

It felt funereal, this impending parting between two friends, but Levi held his feelings in check.

"You know, I'm going to miss this house." Maggie sighed.

Levi said nothing. *Let her talk.*

"Sure, I have God with me wherever I go, and I know that this world is not my home, but I grew up here." Maggie pointed to the sidewalk beyond the brown grass. "Skinned my knees on that cement over there when I learned to ride my bike. Climbed up that tree over there with my brother and got him grounded."

"Malachi was outdoorsy?" Levi asked. "I would never have known."

"Nowadays he spends a lot of time in his study, preparing sermons, but back when he was a kid, he was kind of wild. Often got into trouble with my parents." She laughed. "Mom said he knew better than to teach a five-year-old to climb trees without a harness and a net to catch us if we fell."

Levi raised an eyebrow.

"That's my mom for you. You haven't met my parents, have you?"

"Once in Miami during a disaster relief. Should I visit them again?" Levi wanted to go there, but Maggie apparently didn't catch his drift.

"And...the day Malachi went to college, I cried. I was only a freshman in high school, but I didn't want him to go clear out of state for school. I missed him terribly, but he was going to Bible college to learn to serve God in a pastoral ministry and I had to let him go."

"Understandably."

"Yet, I lived from school break to school break, waiting for Malachi to come home to spend time with me in this house." She turned away from the window. Stared at the mostly empty living room and beyond, to the small kitchen.

"When I went to college, I decided to pick one in town so that I could commute from home," Maggie said. "Every day I could go to class and still come home to my own room and Mom's home-cooked meals."

Levi tried to recall if Maggie ever told him her family story, but then again, prior to last year, they had only been casual friends in church. In the last year, he had been full of himself and his own worries. He felt sorry now that he had taken up so much of Maggie and Malachi's time—to the point that he had forgotten they also had lives of their own.

"In my sophomore year, God called my parents to serve as missionaries in Europe. Dad quit his job and entered the ministry. Next thing I knew, they were gone—first to training and then to the field—and I didn't see them again for the rest of my college years."

"I know that story." Levi felt good that he had paid some attention to the Jacobs siblings who had taken him in. "Only Malachi showed up at your commencement."

"Right. For the balance of my college life, I came home alone and ate alone. I saved a lot of money not living in campus dorms, but I didn't expect to live alone."

Maggie sat down on her gray armchair. "Midtown Chapel became my family. I kept busy and I was in as many activities as I had time for before and after class. I did everything, from teaching in Vacation Bible School and children's camp to ushering in Christmas plays."

"You majored in communications, so you did put it all to good use." Levi leaned against the breakfast counter. There were still two chairs there.

"God worked it out. I helped to organize college and young adult events. In my senior year, I started volunteering in the women's ministry. When the ministry assistant moved out of state because her husband had a job transfer, it was Mrs. Kim who suggested that I send my resume to Tally. So I had a job waiting for me before I graduated from college."

"That's nice. I didn't know what I was going to do after I graduated from college."

"You had a business administration degree. Is that why you're working at the warehouse?"

"I didn't want to be in the office all day long, so being a warehouse manager works for me. Besides, I met you." He waited to see how Maggie reacted to that.

"And Malachi too," Maggie said.

Levi nodded. "Is Tally how you met the Fitz-patricks?"

"Yeah. They're very nice to me. Even gave me a graduation present. I'll see them again when I move to Lakeside since most of them are there, except for Tally, who lives in the Bahamas now. In fact, I'll be working for Colette, the middle daughter, at Lakeside Resort."

Levi wanted to ask Maggie not to go, but who

was he to stop her? The Maggie he knew didn't make decisions willy-nilly. Surely she had prayed about this move to Florida. He could see why she would want to be with her family, with her parents retiring and all.

"When are your parents arriving in the States?" Levi asked.

"Two days before New Year's Day. They're visiting their old friends now and decided to spend the last Christmas with them—just like what I'm doing this Christmas, celebrating it at the Village."

"Speaking of which, have you picked a present for the white elephant gift yet?"

"No. I've been so busy. They said the maximum price has to be five dollars, right?"

Levi nodded.

"What are you going to bring?"

"I was going to bake some cookies."

"If I pay you, will you bake another batch for me to take as my white elephant gift?" Maggie looked at him in earnest.

"You don't have to pay me. Just give me a hug." Levi stood up, stretched out his arms, waiting.

"I'll give you a winter hug."

"What's a winter hug?" Levi was still waiting.

"It's basically a warm hug, rebranded every month. We do it in the women's ministry when someone comes in for counseling in the winter months. They don't leave without getting a winter hug from Mrs. Kim and me."

"I'm waiting."

"Oh I can't." Maggie sniffed her sweatshirt. "I'm dusty and sweaty."

"I don't care."

"You sure?"

Levi nodded.

"Well, you're taller than I am so let's see how I can do this." Maggie wrapped her arms around his waist and leaned into his chest. She stayed there for a while.

"Tell me you only give this winter hug to women." Levi was warming up.

"You're the first man I've hugged this way." Her voice faltered. "It's also a goodbye hug. Something to remember me by when I'm no longer in Georgia."

She pulled back.

"A little longer, please?" He pleaded.

"That's enough."

"All right." He really wanted more, but he also respected Maggie's space. She could hug him whenever she wanted, but only if she wanted to.

"We've been talking about memories, and if I'm not mistaken, you sound like you're going to miss this place and our church." Levi almost asked her if she'd miss him, but he decided not to push it. Premature, perhaps.

Maggie nodded. Her eyes teared up. "I've been here all my life. I love my job in the ministry."

"So why are you leaving now?"

Maggie didn't answer. She stepped back from Levi and looked away.

"Maggie?"

Silence.

Levi searched everywhere for a box of tissues, but there was none in sight. He went around the counter and tore off a piece of paper towel. Handed it to Maggie, who had returned to her position at the window.

She took it from him, blew her nose.

He almost put an arm around her shoulders, but decided not to. There was no one else in the house, and he'd been trying to avoid any physical contact. She had initiated her winter hug. That was all they could handle at this point.

After a little bit of crying, Maggie shrugged. "Such is life."

She walked back to the living room. "I have ten days to pack the rest of my stuff. Not a lot, since they've hauled away my bed and desk—the table you gave me that used to belong to Aunt Marie."

"I'll help you pack whatever you have left. Mostly books, right?"

"You've done enough, Levi." Maggie went to the refrigerator to get a bottled water. She offered one to Levi.

"What? Are you sending me away now?"

"Maybe I need to do this alone from here on out. I can ask people from church to help me load the U-Haul. You don't need to come by. It's easier this way so I don't have to say goodbye to you."

"Then never say goodbye to me at all, ever." Levi stepped closer. "Why don't I drive the U-Haul for you?"

"How are you going to get back here? Fly?"

"I can do that."

"It costs money."

"I'm willing to pay it since it means I get to see you just a little bit longer."

"I'm not dying, Levi. Just moving on."

"Moving on from what?"

Maggie didn't answer. She checked her phone. "Wow. It's noon. We haven't eaten lunch."

"It's on me."

"No, no. It's on me. You helped me all morning and all last week."

"Because I wanted to. I don't need any payment."

"It's just lunch."

"Okay then." It wasn't for show, but Levi could always adjust himself for Maggie. For other people, he didn't care to, but for Maggie, he was always flexible with his time and schedule.

Since when had this been the case? When had it started?

He couldn't remember. It was a gradual process as he got to know Maggie more. It probably started after Malachi left Atlanta. After he'd left, there were only two people left in their small circle: Levi and Maggie. Levi felt that he had been able to focus on Maggie more.

"You can buy lunch next time," Maggie said. "Today, it's my treat, friend."

"Friend? I've been thinking, Mags…" *Maybe I want to be more than friends.*

"About what?"

She didn't look ready to hear it. "We'll talk later."

"I'll go wash up and change."

"Take your time." He sat down on the armchair that Maggie had vacated.

He surveyed the living room one more time. Stared at the dust in the air.

He made a note to vacuum after they came home from lunch. He knew where the vacuum was. It was the only item belonging to Maggie's parents that they hadn't packed. The rest of their possessions in the house, including everything in the kitchen, were all gone.

Wait. Did I say home? Come home?

Well, in a way, this was like a second home for him in the last three years—more so in the last year and a half, post Soline.

This house was where he could be himself, crack stupid jokes, laugh with Maggie and her brother, eat pizza, and watch the Georgia Bulldogs on television every football season.

How could he say goodbye? He understood what Maggie must feel.

He heard the shower come on in the bathroom that was attached to Maggie's downstairs bedroom.

As small as this house was, the architects had managed to squeeze in four bedrooms: two downstairs and two upstairs. While Malachi had occupied one bedroom upstairs, leaving the other available to house visiting missionaries on furlough, the two downstairs bedrooms were taken by Maggie and her parents.

Maggie had the smaller room, and it was barely the size of a closet. If he were to remodel the house…

Huh? What am I thinking?

He tapped his phone and checked his bank account and savings. If he sold his townhouse in

Dunwoody and took that new job at Christmastown, he could buy this house for Maggie without tapping into his savings.

However, knowing Maggie, she would want to be a part of the process. That was where her organization skills shone. Levi wouldn't want to deprive her of the opportunity to share the cost with him. She would want to have a say-so in the home renovation and remodeling, so why not bring her into the project at the start of it?

They could form a limited liability company, and come up with a name. Maybe Jacobs-Theroux LLC or Theroux-Jacobs LLC or whatever Maggie wanted.

If they had the money to pay cash for the house, that would be ideal. However, neither one of them was rich enough for that. They would have to get a loan, with the value of this property so close to midtown Atlanta. After all, this urban neighborhood had been revitalized.

Lord Jesus, do You think I should buy this house for Maggie?

If the property was too expensive for both of them to buy together, then Levi would have his answer.

If they could afford it, then Maggie wouldn't be sad.

Assuming she was sad because she was moving

out of state. This piece of Atlanta might be a nice little present for her.

Levi texted the real estate agent who had helped him buy his Dunwoody property. He gave her the address to Maggie's house, and asked her to compare house prices in the neighborhood.

If it all worked out, then he and Maggie would always have something in common—if they kept the house for the rest of their lives.

What his cousin had said to him the week before came back to Levi's mind.

I'd hate for you to miss the person right in front of you —if she's God's perfect will for you. If not, you two will part ways when she moves away, and that's the end of it.

Then again, it might not be a good idea to turn their friendship into a business partnership simply because Levi wanted to keep Maggie by his side.

Maggie valued honesty but neither of them had been honest with each other. Perhaps it was time for the artificial barrier of friendship between them to come down.

Levi felt bad about his behavior the last year. If Maggie had developed feelings for him—as he had for her now—then it must have been distressing to her. He had endlessly bugged her to help him get his "dream date." Made her his matchmaker.

She was his best friend, and he had taken advantage of her generosity.

Well, she could have said no.

But she hadn't.

The bedroom lock clicked and the door opened. Maggie came out of the bedroom with her hair damp.

"Don't you need to totally dry your hair so that you don't catch a cold? It's forty-five degrees outside the last time I checked."

Maggie pointed to the window. "It's sunny out. And your truck has a heater."

"Still…"

"Oh boy, you're bossy today."

"Go dry your hair while I vacuum the living room."

"I'm hungry now."

"Five minutes. This is a small room."

Reluctantly, Maggie went back to her bedroom, closing the door behind her. She didn't slam it, so Levi knew she wasn't angry.

Levi ran the vacuum and took his time so that Maggie didn't hurry—if she could hear the vacuum above her hairdryer.

He loved doing things for Maggie, although it had pained him lately to have to help her pack. The more they filled up the moving boxes, the more loss Levi felt as she prepared to move out of his life.

Yes, Cyrus was right. Levi had fallen in love with Maggie, even without knowing it at first, but now fully aware of his own feelings. The clues were everywhere and yet he'd been oblivious.

How had it started?

Levi thought back about the telling evidence that his relationship with Maggie had moved beyond a platonic friendship. How could he not have noticed the signs before?

Firstly, he loved being with Maggie. He was comfortable with her—more than with any other woman in his life, including Aunt Marie when she had been alive. It hadn't always been the case in the three years he'd known Maggie, but acutely so in the last year. Maggie had helped him to get over her ex-girlfriend, and he had gotten to know her well.

He felt sorry that he had made her his match-maker. It had created chaos and confusion in their relationship as best friends. It might have driven Maggie to other men if she had thought there was no hope for her and Levi.

Secondly, he had felt intensifying jealousy every time he saw Maggie spending time with Alden. The last two times were particularly both-ersome to him: at the Village community center and at the Italian restaurant on the Christmas concert night.

Even now, he prayed that Alden wouldn't show up to rob his future bride from him.

Future what?

Thirdly, Levi couldn't help thinking about Maggie's well-being when she had failed to show up at the singles dinner party the other night. When he didn't see Maggie, nothing else mattered to him, not even his faux dream date.

He was sure there were more telltale signs, but those were all he could ascertain as the vacuum cleaner drowned out all further thoughts.

Chapter Fourteen

*L*evi had been extra helpful and extra
sweet this week, and he had paid for
their lunch at Whole Foods, even when
Maggie protested all the way through dessert.

"You want me to owe you, don't you?" Maggie
took a spoonful of the bread pudding and pushed
the bowl to Levi. "All yours."

"I don't want you to leave Atlanta..." Levi
looked at the pudding and then at Maggie.
"Or me."

Maggie stared at him. What did he mean by
that? She waited for him to say more. She knew
that if she waited long enough, he'd come forth
with all the clarifications.

Whole Foods was crowded. The dining tables

were next to the busy checkout counters with only a low wall separating the crowd of Saturday shoppers and their table. There was no privacy.

Maggie wasn't surprised when Levi didn't answer her.

"Let's talk at home," he finally said.

"Home?"

"I mean your house."

Maggie sighed. "Technically, it's my parents' home, but it won't be much longer unfortunately. I've already told you that they want to sell it since they're never coming back to Atlanta."

Levi's phone rang, but he didn't pick it up from the table. It was turned over with the back of the casing facing up. "I'll check my voice mail after our lunch."

"It's okay to take the call. Might be important if someone calls you on a Saturday." Maggie said that because she was curious about the caller.

Levi turned the phone over. Maggie could see a woman's name. Sally.

She decided not to speculate. Both of them had male and female friends. No biggie.

"I'll be right back." Levi went outside the café to take the call.

That told Maggie something. He didn't want her to hear their conversation.

Whatever. She didn't have to care anymore. She was moving away for good.

Maggie checked her own phone. Texted Malachi to tell him that the movers had left.

Levi returned quickly. Said little as he finished dessert.

Maggie sipped water through a straw as she watched him.

"Anything I can help with?" she finally said. "Like I could do one last matchmaking project or something?"

She was halfway joking. Truly she was done with helping Levi find his "one true love" or whoever. Who did that in this day and age? Didn't they have apps for that sort of thing these days?

Jokes aside, Maggie believed that the only person who could find Levi's partner for life was God. Not Maggie or Levi himself or anyone else.

Levi gave her a look that said, "What?"

"Sorry for the mess in the last go-round."

Levi chuckled. "No, the person who needs to apologize is me. I put you through a lot, Mags. I'm very sorry."

Maggie almost shrugged, but his apology was so genuine, she felt that she needed to take it seriously. "Everything is a learning experience in God's economy."

Levi put his fork down in the empty bowl. "I found the person I want to spend the rest of my life with."

Maggie nearly spluttered out water. "Really? Who?"

Could it be Sally, the person who just called him? She was afraid to ask. She wiped her mouth with a paper napkin.

"I'm praying about it so I don't want to scare her," he said quietly.

"Makes sense. Don't be rash." Maggie waited.

"For sure."

"A life partner is possibly the future mother of your children," Maggie added.

"Right. How do you know if someone is the right person for you?" Levi asked. "I've failed in my relationships."

"God will show you," Maggie said as though she had any authority. She didn't, and she knew it, but she had heard enough sermons and read enough Bible to know that God was compassionate and will answer His children. "Pastor Kim preached on knowing God's will and making requests of Him in 1 John 5:14-15."

Maggie swiped her phone and read the verse aloud.

Now this is the confidence that we have in Him, that if we ask anything according to His will, He hears us. And if we know that He hears us, whatever we ask, we know that we have the petitions that we have asked of Him.

"What if God has already shown you, and you ignored Him?" Levi asked. "I mean, speaking for myself, of course."

"My dad—who is a pastor too, as you know—would say that we need to get on our knees and repent before the Lord, and then He will get us back on track. One of his favorite verses is 1 John 1:9."

If we confess our sins, He is faithful and just to forgive us our sins and to cleanse us from all unrighteousness.

"Start over. Reset," Levi said. "I get it."

The server came with the bill, and Levi paid it as he had insisted.

As they walked out of the restaurant toward Levi's truck, Maggie got curious. She had been dealing with Levi's personal life for twenty-two months.

"Do I know her?" She waited for Levi to unlock the passenger side.

He nodded. "You know her very well."

"Oh. Then I can put in a good word for you."

"I'm sure you can."

They were buckling in when Levi answered her carefully. Too carefully, in fact, and made Maggie suspicious.

"Okay. I'll help." Not too happy to help, but she'd do it for Levi's sake. "I'm your best friend, after all."

"Are you?" Levi put the truck in reverse and backed out of the parking lot.

They were on the road before he spoke again. "How can you be my best friend when you're in Florida and I'm in Georgia?"

"Technology, Levi. Video calls. Text messages."

"Not in person."

"You could drive seven hours one way to Lakeside." Maggie didn't expect him to.

"I could." Levi checked the map on phone. "It's not a bad drive. Straight through on I-75. I will if you want me to."

"I was kidding."

"I wasn't."

"Aren't you busy with work and life?" Maggie asked.

"Speaking of work, I haven't told you that my

cousin is expanding Christmastown to the greater Atlanta area, and asked me to submit my resume as the regional warehouse manager."

"Interesting." Another sign that Levi would continue to stay in Atlanta while she would start a new life in Florida. Maggie's eyes teared as she looked away. "When is the grand opening?"

Levi stopped at a traffic light. "He didn't say but I'm guessing July. I think he wants the metro market next Christmas season."

"It's a corporation so they'll pay more, I'm sure."

"Yes, but that's not why I would consider it. I'll only go if the Lord directs me to."

"How do you think the Lord would direct you?" Maggie wiped her eyes.

"Providing for my future family, for example." Levi didn't seem to notice Maggie's angst.

Lord, I have to let him go. Right now, in the name of Jesus, I let Levi go.

Goodbye, Levi.

Oblivious to Maggie's prayer, Levi kept his eyes on the road. "Left fork, we go back to the Village and check out the bazaar. Right fork, we go back to your house. What do you think?"

"I've been so busy these couple of weeks that I haven't had time to check out the bazaar."

Maggie's face brightened. "I guess we have a little bit of time now that the house is cleared and most of the packing and moving are done."

"Left it is." Levi flicked on his turn signal. Traffic picked up as they headed toward Midtown Village which was sandwiched between Fulton and DeKalb counties.

They circled the parking lot a couple of times before they found parking.

"I expected it to be this busy." Levi parked his truck.

The sunny day made this a warmer-than-usual mid-December, but Maggie kept her jacket on because of the wind. She wished she had worn a baseball hat or something because she wasn't at work, and now she would be seen with Levi, their non-relationship on full display.

On the other hand, they would probably be in a crowd of strangers and nobody cared.

Maggie waited for Levi to lock his truck. He came around the hood.

Maggie was walking down the sidewalk toward the first booth when she felt a warm hand on hers.

Startled, she looked down.

It was Levi's hand.

"What are you doing?" Maggie asked.

"I'm holding my best friend's hand. Is that not allowed?" He grinned. Charming.

"We're not kids." She pulled her hand away.

"We held hands on the night of the Christmas concert last week, remember?"

"That was because you wanted to show Soline sitting in the balcony that you've moved on. I was basically one of the props on stage."

"Props? That never crossed my mind."

"Oh?" Maggie got curious. "Was it the crowd then? I was pushed back and we almost got separated."

Levi nodded. "Yeah, I didn't want to lose you then."

That was a loaded statement.

"And I don't want to lose you now." Levi reached for her hand again. Wove his fingers into hers.

"What are you trying to tell me?"

Levi didn't answer. He saw someone. He waved—holding up Maggie's hand with his.

Maggie turned in the direction he was waving. There was Forsythia, not in a chef's jacket—smiling from ear to ear and giving them two thumbs up.

What on earth is happening?

Levi didn't explain—and Maggie badly wanted him to. He walked with her, his hand still in hers, along the sidewalk as they checked out the small booths.

A number of people recognized them and smiled at their interlocking hands. Maggie almost wanted to buy a hat of some kind and maybe a pair of sunglasses to hide under, but the bazaar didn't sell those today.

They stopped at Jacinda's booth, which she shared with another resident of Midtown Village. Maggie knew that they had been crocheting and knitting since the summer.

Jacinda had come a long way since losing her seventeen-year-old son more than two years ago. Since then, she had gone back to school, and now operated a hair and beauty salon. Her friend, Gertrude, was an avid quilter and knitter, who gave the newly minted entrepreneur a new knitting hobby.

Jacinda saw Maggie and instead of saying "Merry Christmas!" she said, "You go, girl!"

"These are so pretty." Maggie picked up a knitted crossbody bag. It was in a few shades of teal. "I like this. Oh, you have it in tangerine too. Mom's favorite color. Okay, I want both of these."

Maggie was about to take out her purse from her shoulder bag. Levi stopped her.

"I got this." He swiped his card.

Jacinda made a silent "ooh" with her lips. "Office romance, I see."

"We're not—"

Levi cut her off. "Technically, we're in different departments and don't work in the same office. She's in the women's ministry and I'm in the warehouse."

"Same church." Jacinda cooed. Then she got busy helping another customer.

"Why did you cut me off?" Maggie asked as they walked away.

"I'm trying to send you a message, but you don't seem to get it yet." Levi stepped on the lawn, its dry grass the color of winter brown. They were standing by the tall Christmas tree.

"What message?" Maggie wanted him to spell it out clearly. She didn't want to guess.

"The man you love is loving you back," he whispered softly in her ear.

Maggie couldn't breathe.

The man you love is loving you back.

"I never said a word." Maggie's eyebrows knitted together.

"You don't have to. I can see that you care for me and you cry for me."

"So?" Maggie tried to keep her voice calm. "Not leading indicators."

"But it's true, isn't it? You do have feelings for me." He held her hands.

Maggie felt the warmth of Levi's hands and how their fingers fitted like they belonged together.

She couldn't speak, but Levi continued talking.

"I thought something was developing between us, but I denied myself the happiness of knowing you as more than just my best friend. I thought we had a good friendship and that was enough for me...until it wasn't." He squeezed Maggie's hands gently.

"I gather that you've prayed about this." It was all Maggie could think of to say.

This was coming at her more suddenly than she'd expected, and sadly, only ten days before her departure for Florida.

"If God wants to bless me with you, who am I to say no?" Levi asked. "I'm truly sorry that I didn't see who God had in store for me sooner—but better now than before you leave town."

"I don't know what to say, Levi."

"Cyrus and even Forsythia thought that you and I were already an item. I mean, I didn't tell them that I have the keys to your house and drop in often, and that we are comfortable with each other. That would be TMI."

Was it too much information? To be sure, it was highly unusual, but Levi knew that he had the house keys because Malachi trusted him. Since Malachi trusted him, so did Maggie.

And here we are today.

Maggie could hardly look at him. It had been a long journey for her. She had fallen in love with Levi when she was nursing his broken heart after he witnessed Soline's first love propose to her at Tally's wedding reception in February of the year before. However, with her brother around, Maggie kept her feelings to herself.

After Levi had felt better and gone back to his life without Soline, Maggie thought she had a chance, but then Levi set his sight on anyone but Maggie.

Even though she did her best as Levi's friend, her heart couldn't take it any longer. When her parents told her that they were retiring to Florida and wanted to sell their Atlanta home, Maggie took the opportunity to make a clean break from Levi.

"Now I want us to be more than friends," Levi said.

"More?"

Levi nodded.

"How much more?"

"For starters, this much..." Levi planted a gentle kiss on her forehead.

Maggie was processing his public display of

affection before she realized that he wasn't done communicating.

"And this much…" Levi leaned down, and his lips found hers.

Right in the middle of the afternoon crowd in the Village square.

Chapter Fifteen

hile Levi's feelings for Maggie had developed later than hers, she had not rejected him when he kissed her forehead and then lips, back at the Christmas Village square three afternoons ago.

He thought the crowd had largely ignored them showing a public display of affection. However, the PDA wasn't for them. It was for Maggie. Levi wanted her to know that he wasn't afraid to publicly declare his commitment to her.

That he was serious about it.

Levi replayed the scene over and over again in his head the next three days at home and at work at the warehouse. He had sorted out the inventory himself and didn't need Maggie's help at all—

contrary to what Mrs. Kim suggested the night of the tree lighting.

Mrs. Kim—bless her heart—was full of ideas. Most of them were great ideas that improved the church. But this interdepartmental cross training was something that Levi wasn't sure he could endorse. He didn't mind having workers from other church departments and ministries lending a helping hand in the warehouse, but he was afraid that he'd be called to the Midtown Chapel building to do things like planning children's programs.

Sure, he'd like to have children in the future, but there was always a time for everything under the sun, and now wasn't it.

At this moment, he had a feeling that Maggie was still in a daze about his feelings for her since it might seem sudden. He had to assure her that Theroux men made decisions very quickly. She could ask Cyrus, who knew with God-given certainty that he wanted to marry Amy.

Marry?

He and Maggie hadn't even gone out on their first date.

Sure, they had gone out to eat many times, just the two of them, but a real date night hadn't happened yet. So far both of them had been super busy with work. He had hardly talked to Maggie since church on Sunday.

They were down to her last week at Midtown Chapel. Mrs. Kim hadn't hired a replacement assistant. However, Maggie had spent most of the last days in meetings with Bina and Erika at the Village.

Will Levi hear from Maggie before Christmas?

It was now an hour before the end of the business day on Tuesday. Levi decided to be brave and text Maggie.

LEVI

How's work?

She didn't reply for a good forty minutes.

MAGGIE

Handover complete. My work at Midtown Village—with its four months of Christmas activities—is now officially over.

LEVI

I'm surprised you did that much work. Puts my warehouse job to shame.

MAGGIE

We are each called differently. All I can say now is that my time here is done.

What did she mean by that? Was Maggie

fooling herself? Was she still running away from Atlanta when all arrows were pointing back to Midtown Chapel?

They'd sort it all out this evening.

Maggie was too tired to go out to eat in a restaurant. She wanted to kick back and relax in her pajamas at home. She was very much a homebody.

Levi offered to pick up a Chinese takeout dinner and meet her at her house.

Five o'clock came quickly, and Levi made the call. He left his office in a hurry but was still caught in the Atlanta rush hour, trying to get from his favorite Chinese restaurant to Maggie's house. A ten-minute drive turned into twenty minutes because of a wreck on his side of the street.

Whenever Levi was caught in traffic, it was time to pray.

As was the Theroux tradition of making quick decisions, Levi decided that Maggie was the one. Still, he had to be careful not to push her one way or another or she might misunderstand.

Yes, he was willing to go through life with her, for better or for worse.

When he had found out that Maggie was moving out of town, Levi didn't want her to go.

Still, she was set on leaving, as if the train was revving to go—in potentially the wrong direction

—and nobody could stop it. She had already rented the U-Haul. Malachi and their parents were expecting her.

They had been in the mission field, so surely they understood the importance of listening to God when He changed their course.

But Maggie.

Stubborn Maggie.

Levi wondered how things might have changed had he realized his feelings sooner. Maggie might still be working at Midtown Chapel.

Levi wasn't sure what he could do to make Maggie change her mind and stay in Atlanta. It seemed that the trajectory of her career had been set, and there was no turning back now, right?

"Lord, if her plans are fixed, should I go with her?" Levi prayed aloud. "I'm sure I can find a job in Lakeside. If I can't find any opportunity in the small town, then I'll look in the surrounding big cities."

No one else was in the truck, so Levi continued to talk with God aloud. "On the other hand, I could stay here in Atlanta and work at Christmastown."

He'd earn more income if he worked for Cyrus as his regional warehouse manager. He wondered if Cyrus would agree to let him take alternate Fridays off so that he could make the seven-hour drive to Lakeside, Florida, to see Maggie.

His girlfriend.

It would be a shame for them to part ways merely days after confessing that they had fallen in love with each other.

Before Levi reached Maggie's house, he received a text from Sally, asking him if he had decided to hire her brokerage to represent him in the purchase of the Jacobs family home.

Yet another thing to talk to Maggie about.

Levi wasn't sure if Maggie could handle the extra decision burden after a long day. However, they had to discuss these things before Maggie left town the week after Christmas.

If Maggie was sure God had called her to Lakeside, then Levi would be more than happy to drive the U-Haul truck for her.

However, he wondered if Maggie wasn't the one who was forcing herself to make this sudden change in her career. Perhaps this whole exercise was not from God.

Levi pulled onto Maggie's driveway. Before he could get out of his truck, Maggie opened the garage door and came out in a wool coat. Levi could see the Georgia Bulldogs pajama pants underneath the coat.

"Took you long enough. I'm starving." Maggie

opened the passenger side door and picked up the plastic takeout bag.

"It might be heavy. Let me do it." Levi came around the truck.

"I'm fine. It's not too heavy. Just two dishes, soup, and rice. I can carry this." She walked back toward the garage. Then stopped. "Thank you, Levi, for getting us dinner."

"Welcome." Levi locked the old truck, and then followed Maggie into the house.

The garage led to the old kitchen, where Maggie had prepared two plates, two bowls, and two sets of silverware on the breakfast counter.

She put the plastic bag on the counter and took out what they ordered. "Wash your hands and we can eat."

Levi washed his hands in the sink, looking out through the window at the square-foot garden, now barren. In the spring, there would be herbs, vegetables, and sometimes flowers growing out of those squares. He recalled watering the plants and weeding the garden when Maggie and Malachi had been too busy.

Once this house was sold, he couldn't do that anymore.

Levi dried his hands on a hand towel by the refrigerator. He hugged Maggie from behind.

"Let's do this," he said.

Maggie raised an eyebrow at him. "What?"

"Let's buy this house."

Maggie put a serving spoon in the container of rice. "You and me?"

"Yes, me and you. We can discuss it over dinner." Levi decided that if Maggie was interested at all, he'd introduce her to his real estate agent and see what Maggie thought.

Maggie sat down next to Levi. "Let's say grace first and ask God for wisdom. You pray."

"Lord Jesus, we come before You today. We want to be transparent, with all our problems laid bare before You," Levi prayed. "Bless this food to the nourishment of our bodies, and give us wisdom in every area we're concerned about, including whether we should buy this house. In Your holy name, I pray. Amen."

They started eating the crab meat soup before Levi said more. "If we combine my job at the church warehouse and your job at Lakeside Resort, we might be able to get a loan to buy this house from your parents at market price. We won't need a big loan because I'll sell my townhouse in Dunwoody."

"Then your contribution to this project would be more than fifty percent. I have some small savings, but I don't think it's a good idea to empty out my bank account to put into a house that's built in the fifties."

"I know what you mean. I have some inheritance money but we might need that for future things. Rainy day and all that."

"Right. I've checked the recent sales in this area, and these houses are over half a million dollars if renovated. My parents did some repainting but most of the house is still stuck in the fifties, as you can see." Maggie waved her hand. "If I were to buy this house, I'd gut the interior and redo it to be more modern and open. I'd also change the windows because the insulation is not that great."

"The home inspector would be able to tell us what else is wrong with a house this old."

"It crossed my mind to ask my parents if I could rent-to-own. But that was before I found out that Colette's assistant left to stay at home with her kids." Maggie stirred the soup in her bowl. "I kept thinking that I've prayed about this so many times. I understand that getting out of the boat involves risks, but I am willing to take a step of faith forward."

"If this is really what God wants you to do." Levi put a few scoops of chicken over rice on his plate.

"So far I'm afraid to backtrack. I was sure I felt peace, you know?"

"Did you check the pros and cons?"

"And prayed over every single one of them. Still, I was thinking that I am missing something and I can't put my thumb on it. I've already quit my job as a ministry assistant... Oh." She paused.

"Oh what?"

"I forgot to tell you. A couple of Fridays ago, Mrs. Kim told me about the restructuring of the women's ministry for next year. Instead of putting everything under the women's ministry banner and getting everyone confused about whether the event is for single women, mothers, single mothers, divorced mothers, you name it, Mrs. Kim wants to name each specific sub-ministry. For example, Midtown Moms will become an entity."

"Interesting. So?"

"So they need an event coordinator. That used to be Tally's job and I was sort of her understudy since I worked with her for five years. Mrs. Kim asked that I consider applying for the event coordinator job. She seems to indicate that I have a chance of getting it due to my qualifications and experience."

Levi chewed the chicken slowly, mulling over this new piece of information. God was certainly at work, but Maggie wasn't seeing it.

"What if God has opened that door for you at Midtown?" Levi asked.

"The timing is so off."

"How so?"

"I was thinking, why didn't God open that door before I quit my job?"

Levi shrugged. "Who can know the mind of God?"

"But don't we have the mind of Christ?" Maggie asked.

"Let's see what 1 Corinthians 2:16 says." Levi tapped his phone and found it.

For "who has known the mind of the Lord that he may instruct Him?" But we have the mind of Christ.

"I see quotes around the phrase 'who has known the mind of the Lord that he may instruct Him?' Do you know where it might have been from?" Levi asked.

"Has to be the Old Testament. Let me look it up." Maggie checked her Bible app. "Found the closest reference. Isaiah 40:13."

Who has directed the Spirit of the Lord,
Or as His counselor has taught Him?

"In both verses, the Bible is saying that are in

this earthly body filled with a sin nature, so we can't tell God what to do," Levi said.

"However, Christ in us can show us what we need to do."

"Exactly." Levi nodded. "We need to be willing to change on a dime if the Lord calls us here or there."

"Did God not call me to Lakeside?"

"Or did you hear yourself? What were you running away from?"

Maggie didn't answer. She ate quietly. When she finished her stir-fried beef, she turned to Levi.

Tears in her eyes. "I was running away from you. I thought you didn't want me."

Oh. No wonder she had been looking hurt for weeks.

"I didn't know I did until I realized that the things I've done lately have been to fight for you and for your attention. I hated it when you and Alden got along so well. I didn't like it when you decided to move away. I want you to be by my side always for the rest of my life. I don't think that will work if we're only best friends. I don't want you to date—or worse, marry—someone else."

That was a mouthful but he was being honest with Maggie.

"It took me a while to realize that I was falling in love with you and denying it." He reached for her hand. "Now we're on the same page where our hearts are concerned, but not where our house is."

"I've never been in a long-distance relationship, so I don't know how easy or hard it will be for us."

"I'd rather have you here with me so that I can hold you."

"I didn't know your love language is physical touch," Maggie said. "I thought it was acts of service."

"It is mostly, but every now and then I want a hug—especially from the people I love."

"And what's mine?" Maggie asked.

It looked like she had missed what he just said about the people he loved.

"I think it's quality time," Levi answered him.

Maggie smiled.

"See, we know a lot about each other, but I don't believe we would have if we hadn't spent so much time together, in person, in town. If we only see each other once or twice a month, we will hardly know each other."

"Once or twice a month? What do you mean?"

"It means I'm willing to drive seven hours one way to Lakeside to see you, but due to work, I can only do that every other week or once a month."

"That will get old very quickly and might affect your health."

"For sure."

Maggie refilled her plate with seconds. "This Szechuan chicken is not bad. Not as spicy as I expected."

"They probably toned it down for the American palate."

"I believe you."

They ate quietly for a bit.

Levi prayed that he would say the right words to help Maggie make the right decision. It had to be soon because the U-Haul would arrive in six days.

"Does the event coordinator position at Midtown pay more than the ministry assistant job?" Levi asked.

"It's the women's event coordinator, not a church-wide coordinator." Maggie nodded. "Mrs. Kim suggested I contact HR, and I did, out of curiosity. Yes, the pay is on the level of a new director."

"So if you work in that position at Midtown and I work as the regional warehouse manager at Christmastown, we could pool our income together and buy this house."

"Tell me more."

"We would create an LLC and split the profit

between us. This could be our joint investment property."

"And we don't have any unequal yoke between us since we're both Christians. Hmm." Maggie got up and put her plate in the sink. She leaned back against the counter and surveyed the house. She was facing Levi, and he could tell that she was remembering the history of this place.

If Maggie wanted this house, he'd do everything he could to get her this house.

"Let's back up," Maggie said. "Do we have to buy this house?"

"For your childhood memories?"

"I have those in videos and photographs."

"This house might be old, but it's well built— and only ten minutes to Midtown Chapel."

"It will be a lot of work to renovate this house. However, we might not be able to afford to buy it in the first place unless my parents dropped the price to a range that we can afford."

"Which might make the neighbors unhappy if they think their houses have been devalued."

"If we were to buy this house, we would save it from other people who might not appreciate its history," Levi said. "Down the road from here and a couple of streets over are new houses built on existing old lots. This property could end up being a tear-down lot and the charm of this house would be lost forever."

Maggie smiled. "Seems like you are more attached to this house than I am."

"Well, I have happy memories in this house with you and Malachi."

"In that case, no harm getting a real estate agent to help us process these options."

"I have just the person. She was my agent when I bought my Dunwoody house. I'm not attached to that house, and I'd rather live near Midtown Chapel. I think you and I like the urban lifestyle."

"Wait. You're moving into this house? We can't be roommates."

"We could get married," Levi blurted and instantly regretted it.

"You're funny." Maggie laughed.

She didn't know how serious Levi was. He should tell her about his other uncle who lived in Alaska. He proposed and married his wife three weeks after they met. That was a Theroux record. Levi couldn't break it since he'd known Maggie for three years.

He wondered if Maggie was still trying to wrap around the fact that they were now dating each other. It was too soon to talk about marriage.

Maggie went on. "If we buy this house as an

investment property, then neither of us could live here. We'd rent it out for profit. So where are you going to live? What about me?"

"Didn't I just solve the problem?" Levi asked. Take two.

Maggie didn't reply.

I guess she still doesn't get it.

"Instead of working at Midtown Chapel, if I proceed as planned and move to Lakeside, I'd have a place to stay. If we can get a loan for our business investment without touching your Dunwoody house, then you also have a place to stay. The rent alone for this house will make the house payments each month, plus make us a profit."

Levi's heart sank. Maggie was still talking about Lakeside.

All indicators said to Levi that she had made a rash decision to quit her job that she loved very much. Nonetheless, Levi didn't want to tell her what to do because he didn't want her to blame him if something went south. He decided that the best way for him to help Maggie was to pray for her fervently and let God sort out her career for her.

Levi sighed. "Let's call my agent and ask for a meeting while you're still in town. She can show us all the possible options for our LLC."

"Our LLC. We still need a name."

"I love you," Levi said.

"That's not a good name. I Love You LLC? Seriously, Levi."

Levi didn't know what to think. Maggie was a smart lady who rarely missed the point, but now she seemed to be losing her ability to parse logic. Perhaps she was nervous in front of him. When was the last time Maggie had been nervous in front of him?

"Call your agent, Levi."

Levi called but she wasn't there. He left a message for Sally.

"Sally? Her name is Sally?" Maggie asked after he hung up.

"Yes."

"Didn't you talk to her last Saturday? She called you while we were at lunch."

"You don't miss anything, do you? How did you know who I talked to last Saturday?"

"I saw it on your phone when you took the call."

"Your eyesight is amazing."

"I happened to look in that particular direction."

Her explanation sounded logical. Levi wasn't sure if Maggie was the jealous type, like he was. He had tried to keep his own jealousy in check. As long as Alden stayed away from Maggie, Levi would have less stress.

"So let's pray about this some more and see where God leads us," Levi said. "I'm open to God's directions because His ways are higher than my ways."

"I know that verse. Isaiah 55:9." She even had it memorized.

For as the heavens are higher than the earth,
So are My ways higher than your ways,
And My thoughts than your thoughts.

"You know your Bible, Maggie."

"This is because I grew up at Midtown Chapel where we had—and still do—solid Bible studies and Bible sword drills. My youth was filled with church life. I almost went to Bible college like my brother, but the Lord directed me to study communications instead."

"Doesn't that remind you of the verse that Pastor Kim mentioned a few weeks ago?" Levi almost read the verse aloud from his Bible app, but Maggie beat him to it because she also had Proverbs 16:9 memorized.

A man's heart plans his way,
But the Lord directs his steps.

"That verse also applies to our situation with this house and with our careers." Maggie cleared Levi's plates and started loading the dishwasher.

"We have discussed multiple scenarios," Levi put away the leftovers in the refrigerator. "Let's pray over all of them because we have to choose one."

"If God leads me to Lakeside, will you accept it?" Maggie asked as she watched Levi wiped down the countertop.

"If we are sure He is, then I'll move to Lakeside too."

"What if you have to be in Atlanta and I have to be in Lakeside?"

"Ideally, we would both stay in the same city. I'd rather not have a long distance relationship across two states, you know?"

"Maybe not permanently, but for some months?"

Levi thought about soldiers on deployment overseas away from their spouses stateside. They had it harder than seven hours of driving between him and Maggie.

"I'll have to endure the separation."

Yes, he'd have to.

As long as God was in it, Levi knew he could endure it.

Chapter Sixteen

"Have you ever driven on a road, missed your exit, and heard your GPS tell you to please make a U-turn?" Pastor Kim walked back and forth on the raised platform that connected the lectern to the choir loft. He stopped at the edge, where a row of potted red poinsettias had been arranged.

The row of poinsettias stretched all the way to the front of the orchestra section, the grand piano, and ended at the door where the choir had left after they finished singing the last Christmas carol, which still echoed in Maggie's head because it was loud.

Normally, she'd sit further back in the sanctuary. However, she had carpooled with Levi, who had run late due to Christmas Eve traffic in Dunwoody. As it was with Midtown Chapel tradition, if you arrived at church late, you ended up sitting in the front rows if you couldn't find anyone to save you the prized back row seats.

Still, there was no better place to be for Maggie than right here in church on Christmas Eve, which fell on a Sunday morning this year. Maggie loved being in church. She felt at home in church.

"Life can be filled with wrong roads, potholes, U-turns, endless detours, and dead ends, as we all know. How is this a Christmas message? Stay awake and you'll find out. Let's pray."

Maggie bowed her head, and she assumed that sitting next to her, Levi also did.

"Father God in heaven, thank You for another Christmas season when we commemorate Your birth as a perfect, sinless human, the Lamb of sacrifice who would, thirty-three years later, carry the sins of the world to the cross. Remind us this Christmas what You have done for us, and may we never take for granted the reason for the season: our Lord and Savior, Jesus Christ. Hallelujah. In Your holy name, I pray. Amen."

"Amen," Levi and Maggie said simultaneously, along with the rest of the congregation.

"Turn with me to Matthew 1:21." Pastor Kim opened his own Bible.

Maggie was happy that Levi had brought a printed Bible and did not open his phone app instead. She found herself comparing Levi with Alden. She had seen Alden in Sunday school, flipping between his Bible app and text messages on his phone. Perhaps Alden had been able to split his focus in the Bible study, but small things like that would be a turn-off for Maggie.

Levi glanced her way and smiled.

Maggie turned her attention to her own Bible and the sermon booming into her ears. Something must be wrong with the sound this morning. Perhaps the usual sound guy was out of town, and the backup sound guy had technical difficulties calibrating the decibels.

"Where are you heading in life?" Pastor Kim asked. "Are you precisely where you need to be? Are you getting there? Or are you never going to get there?"

The screen behind the pastor displayed Matthew 1:18-23.

"Let's all stand for the reading of God's Word," Pastor Kim said.

Maggie held her Bible, her notebook, and her pen in her hands and stood up. Levi dropped his pen, but Maggie couldn't help him with it because her hands were full.

After they had read the passage aloud, Pastor Kim prayed, and the congregation sat down.

"In this sermon, we're going to break down this passage, and then you can go home and have a real merry Christmas, being at peace with God and yourself." Pastor Kim put a finger on his open Bible. "Let's begin with Matthew 1:18."

Now the birth of Jesus Christ was as follows: After His mother Mary was betrothed to Joseph, before they came together, she was found with child of the Holy Spirit.

"Point number one: Get on the right road. Matthew 1:18 says that Joseph and Mary were engaged to each other. They were preparing for their wedding. After the wedding they would have kids. Mary did not expect to be pregnant before her wedding day. The events were out of order. It seemed like she and Joseph had gotten on the wrong road. What now?"

Maggie underlined the phrase "right road" in her notebook. What was God saying to her? Had she been on what she thought was a wrong road? Staying in Atlanta, for example. What was so wrong about that? Why did she have to leave if she loved this place, this church, and her work so much?

"We have a number of engaged couples in our church. They're looking forward to a life together as husband and wife, who will eventually start new families. Everyone that my wife, Lydia, and I have talked to about their wedding day told us that they want everything to go smoothly. They don't want anything to go wrong. But what if something does go wrong? Be careful about this question. Is the road you think is wrong really wrong?"

If Maggie moved to Lakeside, would she be heading in the right direction? Was that lakeside town where she needed to be? Would God have sent her there just as He had sent the Fitzpatrick family and Malachi, and now Mom and Dad?

Maggie looked over at Levi, who was also taking notes. His handwriting was better than hers. Her heart warmed. This was all she wanted on Christmas Eve. Go to church with Levi. Sit in church and listen to a good sermon. Spend time with God and with each other.

"Point number two: Stay the course that God has set for you." Pastor Kim surveyed the sanctuary. "Even though the Bible says that Mary was carrying a special baby who was given to them by the Holy Spirit, Joseph still thought there was something wrong with the situation. Matthew 1:19 was his human solution."

Then Joseph her husband, being a just man, and not wanting to make her a public example, was minded to put her away secretly.

"Joseph planned to send Mary away and hide her so that nobody would know about the out-of-wedlock baby. He wanted to take a U-turn back to the beginning where he could have a do-over. Reboot the situation. Reset the clock. With Mary out of sight, it was like everything was fine."

Pastor Kim's words made Maggie think. Relocating to Lakeside would look like she was starting over and rebooting her life, but she could never get rid of the pain in her heart. Thankfully, she was on the other side of this pain now since her love for Levi was no longer unrequited, but she still had this whole unresolved situation before her: she was moving next week to Lakeside, away from Levi.

"So far we have seen that Mary and Joseph had an unexpected situation they felt that they had to solve on their own. Joseph was about to take matters into his own hands with his own human solution," Pastor Kim said. "Let's see how God corrected Joseph's perspective in Matthew 1:20."

But while he thought about these things, behold, an angel of the Lord appeared to him in a dream, saying, "Joseph, son of David, do not be afraid to take to you Mary your wife, for that which is conceived in her is of the Holy Spirit.

"Point number three: Focus on God's calling for your life. Joseph's calling is to be the head of his household as the husband to Mary and the earthly father to the holy child of God. God has placed Joseph there for such a time as that." Pastor Kim lifted his Bible in the air. "Each of us has a calling. Find out what your calling is and follow God's lead. Whatever God calls you to do, stick to it—assuming you do know what your calling is. Even if you don't see the end of it, stick to it. God has a plan that He may not reveal to you right now."

Maggie wondered how she was going to stay in the calling of God when she started work in January at Lakeside Resort. The company might be owned by a Christian family, but that was all. For many years now, Maggie had been sure that she was meant to work in a church and do ministry work in a church setting. Had she heard it wrong?

She could always work or volunteer at Lakeside Chapel, where her brother was. However, as far as she was concerned, she hadn't heard a clear call from God for her to find work at Lakeside Chapel. She planned to be a member of that church, yes, but when she moved to Lakeside, her day job would be at the resort. She would spend all her time promoting the resort and its many amenities. She would assist Colette in making the daily administrative work efficient and productive so that the company would make a profit every year. Was this her new calling?

Pastor Kim walked back and forth on the platform. "To Joseph's benefit, the angel revealed God's plan to him. He got the preview, so to speak. Read Matthew 1:21 with me."

And she will bring forth a Son, and you shall call His name Jesus, for He will save His people from their sins.

"My Lord, my Savior," Maggie whispered to herself. A prayer arose in her heart. She knew that she would rather promote her Redeemer than a resort. Not all Christians were called to work in a church. However, Magdalene Grace Jacobs was.

She was also certain about another thing: God had gifted her with an organizational skill that she had used in the women's ministry. That ministry had now expanded to encourage Christian women everywhere, locally and abroad. The empty event coordinator seat had to be filled.

To be sure, God could take care of any ministry without Maggie's help. God did not need Maggie. However, God had invited Maggie to join Him in the kingdom work to minister to women of all ages, mothers and daughters, grandmothers and granddaughters. It would be her loss if she said no.

"Matthew 1:21 is an oft-quoted Christmas verse that reminds us that we can start over with Christ." Pastor Kim put his hand on his Bible. "Christmas reminds us why Jesus came. We have a sin problem, and God has a Savior solution. His name is Jesus, and 'He will save His people from their sins.' He has saved me from my sins. What about you?"

Yes, Maggie had also accepted Jesus as her Lord and Savior for the remission of her sins and the gift of eternal life. She knew that Levi was also a believer, like she was. He had taken a large pay cut to work at the church warehouse because he, too, wanted to serve God. However, his calling was different from Maggie's. When his cousin offered him a job at Christmastown, he could also serve God there in the Christian company. Therein was the difference between their callings.

No two callings were exactly alike. If God

called Levi to leave the church warehouse and go work at Christmastown, then he should go. If God called Maggie to stay put at Midtown Chapel, then she should stay. No matter what her feelings were, she had to "stick to it," as Pastor Kim said.

I get it now.

"If you're stuck in a pothole, or the wrong road, or dead ends, the three points I gave you will not work if you do not have Jesus. Read Matthew 1:22-23 with me, and we'll be done." Pastor Kim read the verse aloud.

> *So all this was done that it might be fulfilled which was spoken by the Lord through the prophet, saying: "Behold, the virgin shall be with child, and bear a Son, and they shall call His name Immanuel," which is translated, "God with us."*

"I can preach a whole sermon on this one verse alone, but tonight I want you to see that Jesus is also called Immanuel. This name of Jesus means 'God with us.' That is, God is with you if you have Jesus. If God is with you, you can climb mountains, overcome Goliaths, have a fulfilling purpose, and live a life of peace, especially peace with God."

Pastor Kim closed his Bible. "Wandering down

the wrong road? Come home to Christ. Hit a dead end where it's all a pit of despair? Look to Jesus, your lifesaver. Let's pray."

Maggie closed her eyes and listened to what she had expected to be a short prayer.

"Thank You, Heavenly Father, for sending Your only begotten son, Jesus Christ, to come down to earth to save us from our sins. We chose this time of the year to commemorate His earthly birth, but let us not forget why He came at all: to save us from our sins. Thank You for this Christmas season. May it always be Christmas in our hearts as we sing with joy that 'the Lord has come.' In the precious name of Jesus, I pray. Amen."

When Pastor Kim finished praying, Maggie opened her eyes. The choir and orchestra had returned to their places on the platform, all dressed in Christmas colors.

"If you're visiting our church, I invite you back on Resurrection Sunday in the spring. We will talk some more about what happened when Jesus Christ went to the cross, was buried, and rose again on the third day." On that note, Pastor Kim stepped off the platform.

Maggie knew what was coming and she grabbed Levi's arm.

"My favorite moment!" Maggie whispered in his ear. She wanted to say more, but the orchestra was about to begin. She had enjoyed this every Christmas. If Midtown Chapel stopped singing this oratorio, she would go downtown to the Atlanta Symphony Orchestra to hear it.

"I know," he whispered back.

That told Maggie that he remembered last Christmas, or even the two other Christmases before that.

They smiled at each other as the music director led the choir and orchestra in an uplifting rendition of George Frideric Handel's *Messiah* oratorio.

As the pipe organ reverberated in the sanctuary, the "Hallelujah" chorus broke out, and everyone stood up to sing along. When it was over, they cheered and clapped.

Maggie sat down again to put away her pen in her purse, and the Bible and notebook in her tote bag.

Silently, her heart began to pray.

Forgive me, Lord, for I have strayed. In my attempt to solve my problems myself, I walked by my own feelings and not by faith in You. I started to take the road not meant for me, toward endless detours ahead of me. Thank You for stepping in just in time to rescue me before I hit a dead end.

You put me back on the right path. Protect my calling, Lord. Preserve my soul. Teach me to walk by faith in You from now on for the rest of my life. In Your holy name, I pray. Amen.

Yes, Midtown Chapel was the church she wanted to attend. The women's event coordinator position was the job she wanted to do. And Levi Theroux sitting next to her was the person she wanted to be with.

All three elements of her life right now were here in Atlanta.

Maggie felt that God had cleared the air for her. Oh, so many things had happened this month. She'd have to take some time to properly praise God for all the good things He had done for her or brought her way or shown her.

She knew she had to eat the humble pie and call Colette on Monday to apologize for changing her mind about moving to Florida. Being a Christian herself, Colette would surely understand that God's ways were always above human ways, as it was written in Isaiah 55:9 that she and Levi had discussed a few days ago.

In fact, there was no reason Lakeside Resort couldn't host some of the regional women's events that she would be organizing with Mrs. Kim for Midtown Chapel, not just for Midtown Moms but for the women's ministry as a whole. It would open the doors to using Lakeside Resort as the retreat center of choice, especially in the winter season. The possibilities were endless. That would probably make her resignation easier for Colette to bear if she knew that repeated business was coming her way.

Maggie would have to find Mrs. Kim and talk to her about adding a new retreat location to their site rotation.

Perhaps in the future Maggie might still move to Florida. But right now, for such a time as this, Maggie knew she was needed at Midtown Chapel to help with the women's ministry. There was much kingdom work to be accomplished yet, and there was a seat in the house of the Lord for her.

Church dismissed and people walked out or stopped to chat with their friends as "Hark, the Herald Angels Sing" filled the sanctuary.

Maggie got up and Levi helped her put her down coat on. Truly she didn't need any help— where was Levi when she had worn the same coat all those years?—but she didn't want to turn him down. It felt nice to have a companion who cared.

It was definitely more interesting to walk through life with someone she loved and who loved her.

As they made their way toward the doors at

the back of the sanctuary, they wished friends and strangers a hearty "Merry Christmas!"

In the lobby, people milled about, taking pictures in front of various Christmas decorations.

"Shall we get a selfie?" Levi pointed to the two-story Christmas tree in the atrium.

"Why not?" Maggie followed him through the crowd.

Volunteers were taking photos for people in a queue. Levi and Maggie had to line up and wait a bit. When it was their turn, Levi handed his phone to an available volunteer, and they stepped toward a spot in front of the Christmas tree.

Levi put his arm around Maggie's shoulders and leaned toward her ear.

"Merry Christmas, sweetheart," he whispered. "Let's serve God together."

Let's serve God together.

Then why did God allow Maggie to resign from church work and then to get a job at Lakeside Resort? Why didn't God send anyone to stop her? Tally could have. Malachi could have. Her parents could have. Even Mrs. Kim could have.

Yet no one did.

Slowly, the reason dawned on her.

It was a test.

Lakeside was a test.

The test would make Maggie answer two questions.

If God calls you to go, would you go?

If God calls you to stay, would you stay?

"Yes, Lord," Maggie whispered softly enough that she was sure nobody heard her but God. "Yes, Lord."

Chapter Seventeen

On Christmas morning, Maggie was sitting at the breakfast counter, drinking hot cocoa with marshmallows on top, and talking to her brother on her tablet. The tablet was sideways on a kickstand on the counter. It was easier that way since there was no coffee table in the living room to hold the tablet. Besides, it had a bigger screen than her phone.

Maggie could see Malachi's face on the gallery view of the video app. One panel showed Maggie and the other panel showed Malachi's live video. His hair was askew, like he had just come out of the shower. But he had shaved nicely and put on a red-and-black buffalo check flannel shirt, as if he was going somewhere.

"You got a better offer," Malachi stated on the video call. His words made it sound like Maggie's employment choice was self-serving.

"Well, the better offer came from God Himself." Maggie wasn't upset with Malachi's response, but her brother was sometimes blunt as blunt can be.

"Have you called Colette?" Malachi leaned back on the couch he was sitting on.

"Tomorrow. I don't know if she's at the office since it's the day after Christmas—even though it should be a workday at the resort—but I'm going to try to reach her," Maggie said. "I hope she understands my situation."

"I'm sure she will. She's more spiritually mature than you think."

Wait. What?

"Are you good friends with Colette?" Maggie asked. Not playing matchmaker, but curiosity got the better of her. Malachi's words made her wonder how he knew Colette that well.

"We're friends at church, if that's what you're asking." Malachi drank coffee and stared at his phone camera that seemed to be on a stand in front of him. He leaned toward the camera. "And that is all. Please, don't try to set us up. It won't work. There is no chemistry between us."

"Oh, you checked."

"I checked. Don't worry about me. I'm happy being a single pastor right now. I might be unmarried for the rest of my life, and I'll be totally happy." He reached for something outside the camera range. It turned out to be a towel. He put that over his head, dried his hair a bit, and then put the towel on the coffee table where the phone apparently was.

"Are you alone this morning?" Maggie asked. It was about nine o'clock, and Levi was picking her up at eleven for their Christmas luncheon at Midtown Village. She had two hours to talk with Malachi and call her parents on their cell phones before she would need to go out.

It was a good thing that she had showered and dressed. That way, she could stay longer on the phone with her family without worrying about not having enough time to get ready.

"Only for this morning. I slept in a bit. Woke up at eight. Read my Bible. Made some coffee." He lifted his coffee mug in the air. "I'm taking it easy and enjoying the peace and quiet in my log cabin for a couple of hours."

Maggie felt bad that she wasn't there to keep her only brother company.

"Later this morning, I'm going to have Christmas brunch with the Fitzpatrick family at Lakeside Resort," Malachi said.

"Good. I don't feel so bad anymore."

Malachi laughed. "I'm older than you by four years, and yet why do I often get the feeling that you want to care for me like I'm your lonely little brother?"

"Because I love you, Mal." Maggie blew him kisses on the screen. She tapped on her screen and hearts filled the video app.

"Sappy, Mags. Stop it." Even as he said it, he laughed, and Maggie knew he enjoyed the display of sibling affection over the video.

"I wish I could be together with you at Christmas," Maggie said.

"But you'd rather be with Levi." A sly smile plastered on Malachi's face.

Maggie didn't say a word. Today was the eighth day of her relationship with Levi. Wasn't it too premature to announce it to her family?

"I already know," Malachi said quietly.

"Know what?"

"About you and Levi. He called me yesterday after church and told me."

"What did he say?" Nothing ventured, nothing gained. She had to ask.

"He wanted to make sure it's fine with me if he dates my favorite sister."

"Your only sister."

"My only favorite sister."

Maggie wondered if Levi should have discussed with her first about what he was going to say to Malachi. Perhaps they could have prepared for the other potential eventuality. "Did he actually say 'fine with you' or were you summarizing?"

"A bit of both. He basically said something like —he found the person he wants to spend the rest of his life with and it's my sister. Is that fine with you?"

"What did you say?"

"I told him I approve—because I like him— but if he hurts you in any way, I'm going to put aside my pastor hat and put on my big brother hat and give him a what's what."

Maggie didn't want to tell Malachi that she had hurt her own self more. All that time she had been in love with Levi and never told him. All that time he hadn't been aware of her love for him. And all that time he made her find a potential girlfriend for him.

Her own angst had caused her to take matters into her own hands. Fleeing Atlanta was her own choice. It was a way for her to avoid having to confront Levi and potentially get rejected.

That one decision had a profound effect on her calling. Then again, abandoning God's call had made her reassess her true calling and caused her to realize her real skillset.

Romans 8:28 all over again.

Maggie couldn't get mad at Levi for not being aware that he loved her too, that everything he'd done for her had been an expression of his love for her. Somehow, he wanted to preserve their friendship. That made Maggie respect him so much. He could be trusted with her house keys because he wouldn't cross the line.

Above all, Malachi trusted Levi, and that said a lot about Levi's character.

It had taken other people, like his cousin Cyrus, to make Levi wake up and realized that if he loved Maggie, he had to do something about it before someone else whisked her away or before she moved out of state and out of sight—as she had almost done.

Maggie thanked God for rescuing their love story in time for Christmas.

If Mom and Dad were here, they would have reminded her of 1 Peter 4:8, a verse that Dad had preached on before.

And above all things have fervent love for one another, for "love will cover a multitude of sins."

Dad had often talked about its related verse, Proverbs 10:12, the one that he had required

Malachi and Maggie to recite when they had immature sibling fights.

> *Hatred stirs up strife,*
> *But love covers all sins.*

Maggie's and Malachi's phones both sounded at the same time. It was a familiar tone.

"Looks like Mom and Dad are initiating a group chat," Malachi said. "All right. I'll hang up now. See you in the family chatroom."

Maggie nodded. She wondered if Malachi had told Mom and Dad about her and Levi. Then again, their parents had been traveling all over the place on their way home for good. Besides, knowing Malachi, he probably left that to her. It's her relationship. She could tell their parents herself.

The four-way video call meant that Mom and Dad were using their own separate phones to log into the chatroom. Maggie's tablet screen split into four quarters, with each of the family members appearing in one quadrant.

"Merry Christmas!" everyone said in unison.

"Wow, we make a good a cappella quartet." Mom seemed to be sitting at an airport terminal.

"Where are you, Mom?" Maggie asked.

"We're at the Charles de Gaulle Airport in Paris."

Dad nodded. "Can't wait to see you at our new log cabin home next week."

Maggie wanted to say something, but Malachi had something else to say first.

"Is your flight on time?" Malachi asked. "I've written down on my calendar that I need to pick you up at the Orlando airport on Wednesday night."

"Wednesday?" Maggie thought it was Tuesday.

"Yeah, we decided to stop in Colorado to see some friends, and then we'll fly to Florida to stay for good," Mom said. "I miss you all so much, but if we don't go ahead and see those friends, we might not see them again for a very long time."

Maggie wondered how two extrovert parents had produced two introvert kids. Even though Malachi was a pastor, he was really an introvert at heart.

As for Maggie, she preferred to work behind the scenes, backstage, and away from the limelight.

However, Mom and Dad were always out there in the spotlight. Pastor Fizz had already said that he wanted Dad to find a third career at Lakeside Chapel. It seemed that Dad wouldn't be totally retiring once he moved to Lakeside. Even if he wasn't on the church payroll, Dad would probably volunteer. He wasn't one who would sit still.

"Sorry we're not there with you on Christmas Day, dearies," Mom said. "However, we're live on video in real time, so all is not lost. It's 4:30 p.m. in Paris, so I'm thinking it's 10:30 a.m. over there?"

"It's actually 9:30 a.m.," Malachi said. "We turned our clock back an hour in November, remember?"

"Did you have a good Christmas in Paris?" Maggie asked.

Dad and Mom nodded simultaneously.

"We stayed with some missionary friends outside Paris," Mom said. "We went to the Christmas Eve service with them last night and then this morning we had crepes for brunch. We exchanged gifts before we left for the airport and here we are."

"How long have you been sitting at the airport?"

"A few hours. Our flight is not until tonight, but there's a charging station here, so we've been calling everyone to wish them a merry Christmas."

Dad nodded as Mom talked. He munched on something that looked like some sort of potato chip.

"When are you going to be in Lakeside,

Mags?" Mom asked. "Are you still going to stay with Malachi and not with us? Our cabin is only next door to his and it's bigger."

"You'll be hosting missionaries on furlough and having Bible studies," Malachi said. "Maggie wants peace and quiet."

"We'll talk about it when we all get to Florida," Dad said.

"About that..." Maggie drew a deep breath. "Lots to tell you, Mom and Dad."

"Good or bad?" Dad asked.

"Romans 8:28."

"Resolved now?"

"Yes. I made a huge mistake, but God corrected it and showed me the path I need to take."

"Psalm 16:9 in action. Now you are ready to tell me what happened and what you learned through the experience." Dad waited.

"Is this going to end up in one of your sermons?" Maggie asked.

Dad didn't reply, which could mean anything in that pastor's mind.

Once a pastor, always a pastor—even when he was retired.

Even so, Dad had never been harsh to Maggie. Mom might get into a southern hissy fit sometimes, but she would calm down as soon as Dad put his hand on her shoulder and said, "Let God take care of it."

This was one of those "let God take care of it" moments.

"Breaking news," Maggie said. "I'm not taking the job at Lakeside Resort. I believe that God has called me to continue serving in the women's ministry at Midtown Chapel in Atlanta. However, I would no longer be the ministry assistant. Mrs. Kim offered me the job of event coordinator instead, which turns out to be something like the deputy director because I assist Mrs. Kim in organizing all the activities and projects she wants to do for the women at church and in the region, and in fact, the world."

"So by 'event,' you really meant projects." Dad ate more chips.

"I suppose. It's a new position so they haven't worked out everything. All I know right now is that I get to do more."

"And they pay you more," Mom said.

"It's a church, so I don't expect them to match Lakeside Resort."

"No, but they still need to pay you decent living wages. Atlanta is a very expensive place to live."

Maggie decided that this wasn't the time to talk to Mom and Dad about buying the house from them. Today she just wanted them to know that she's staying put in Atlanta.

"When God calls you to a place, you stay put until He moves you," Dad said. "You don't move yourself."

"That's my lesson, Dad."

"Very good." Dad was deep in thought while he opened another bag of chips.

"I texted Mrs. Kim this morning to wish her a merry Christmas and to tell her that I have prayerfully decided to take her offer and send in my résumé," Maggie said. "She said that the job is mine and they don't need to interview anyone else. She's considering it a promotion for me."

"But you resigned."

"Right. So she needs the HR to work on reinstating me. The church offices are closed all week, so it will be the second day of January before they get back to the office."

"We will pray about this," Dad said. "If God wants you to have this new job, then He will clear all the obstacles for you and make your path smooth."

"Thank you, Dad."

"Let's pray right now."

Everyone bowed their heads as Dad prayed for God's perfect will to prevail over Maggie's potential new job.

After they prayed, Mom had a question. "Are both of Lydia's kids home for Christmas?"

"Not Oliver. He's still out there somewhere serving the country." Maggie knew that Mrs. Kim's eldest son was a Navy SEAL and that nobody in church knew what he did exactly. "Iseul is home though, waiting for news from her older brother."

"When you see Lydia, tell her that I'm thinking of her and that we should have tea sometime when I go to Atlanta or she goes to Lakeside." Mom reached over and grabbed some chips from Dad's bag. Her hand appeared on Dad's window.

"Will do," Maggie said.

"So you're technically in between jobs?" Malachi asked.

"Looks like it."

"You want to come to Lakeside Chapel and volunteer for a few days?" Leave it to Malachi to recruit volunteers.

"Sure can. I'm driving down to Lakeside tomorrow and will stay until Sunday. Then I have to come home that day after church. I need to rest a day and prepare for my meeting with Mrs. Kim and paperwork with HR on Tuesday."

"I don't want you driving seven hours alone,"

Dad said. "Does anyone else need a few days off who can go with you?"

Maggie thought of Levi, but wasn't sure if the warehouse was open this week. In the past, sometimes they did, sometimes they didn't. All she knew was that the Village was still operational since this was an important business season. Only the main church offices were closed until the new year.

Maggie heard the doorbell. "Hold on a second. Someone's at the door."

She knew who it was, but she hadn't had a chance to tell Mom and Dad about dating Levi. They sort of knew who Levi was—that he was Malachi's friend from church. He was also Maggie's friend, but Malachi had first dibs because three years ago when Levi started working at the church warehouse, Malachi recruited him to go on a disaster relief mission trip when a severe hurricane hit Florida's Emerald Coast.

So, he would always be known as Malachi's friend to Mom and Dad, even though Maggie worked with Levi at church more than Malachi had.

Sure enough, when Maggie checked the security video, she saw that Levi was standing outside. She knew he was coming over to pick her up so they could go to the Christmas luncheon together.

She unlocked the front door to let Levi in.

"Merry Christmas!" He hugged her.

"Merry Christmas—"

Uh oh.

She had forgotten to mute her tablet in the kitchen or face the camera in another direction. She turned and, sure enough, she could see the window—the bottom right quadrant of the split screen—showing her and Levi hugging.

"PDA already?" Malachi's laughter was loud and boisterous. He was slapping his thighs so hard.

"Who is that?" Mom asked rather loudly.

Dad was peering into the camera, as if that helped.

"My family," Maggie said to Levi. "This is how we're celebrating Christmas this year. All remote, all online."

"I'm here in person," Levi whispered in her ear and gave her a quick kiss on her cheek.

"I saw that!" Mom said over the tablet speakers.

Maggie chuckled as she held Levi's hand and led him to the kitchen. She sat down on the chair she had been sitting on. Levi pulled up the other chair next to her.

"Mom and Dad," Maggie said. "You met Levi maybe three years ago at the disaster relief in Miami. Remember?"

Dad nodded. "Yeah, we were on furlough and the hurricane happened. Levi and Malachi cooked for the workers."

"Hello Mr. and Mrs. Jacobs," Levi said. "Merry Christmas."

Dad wished him the same, but Mom didn't reply.

Malachi waved to Levi on his camera. They greeted each other as Maggie tried to figure out how to explain to her parents—especially Mom—about Levi.

She prayed quickly and then decided that the best thing to do was to just tell it as it was.

"Mom and Dad, Levi and I are dating," she said casually.

First, there was silence.

Dad picked up another potato chip or something and nibbled on it. "I guess it's someone we know and whom we've met. He's not a total stranger."

Malachi looked amused, like he was waiting for a shoe to drop.

Maggie dared not look at Mom's panel on the video chatroom.

She glanced over at Levi, who quietly held her hand under the counter. She felt nervous.

Nonetheless, even if Mom disagreed in any

way, it would be hard for Maggie to let Levi go. She had waited a long time for him.

Suddenly Mom clapped like she was at a concert or something. She laughed and clapped again. And then she said the most peculiar thing.

"About time!"

Chapter Eighteen

*W*hen Malachi said he had to go to a luncheon at Lakeside Resort, Maggie took the opportunity to exit the family chatroom as well. She felt relieved that there wasn't any drama from her parents regarding Levi.

He was still sitting there at the breakfast counter, waiting for something.

"Who knew that your participation in the disaster relief in Miami three years ago made an impact on my parents," she said.

"I was impressed by your parents also. They were in their late sixties and still served. We cooked like crazy, I tell you." Levi grinned as he seemed to recall some memories that Maggie wasn't privy to because she hadn't been in Miami.

"Which tells me that they're not really retiring when they move to Lakeside. They will be working for the Lord in some capacity. Pastor Fizz had been recruiting them."

"I'm glad your parents approve of me, and I would like to meet them in person someday."

Maggie had an idea. "Is the warehouse open next week?"

"Yes, actually. We're getting new pop-up houses from Hiroki from tomorrow until Saturday. They're preparing for the second village, remember?"

"Oh bummer. I was thinking that you could come with me to Lakeside if the warehouse is closed."

"Oh well. Another time then. What's your plan like next week?"

"I'll be in Lakeside, visiting my parents and brothers until Sunday after church. Then I drive back to Atlanta."

Levi thought for a bit. "How about I fly to Lakeside on Friday night and then drive back with you on Sunday after church? That way you won't be driving alone both times."

"Wouldn't it be costly? Flights on holidays are expensive."

"Don't worry about that."

"Well, in that case, I could use your company,"

Maggie said. "Dad would be happy to hear about your offer. He had asked me if anyone else would come with me on the road trip."

"You know me, Mags. I will always be here for you."

"Will you?"

Levi nodded. "How long have we known each other?"

"Three years." Maggie wondered what he was getting at. "In the eternal scheme of things, three years are nothing."

"For us mere mortals, three years means thirty-six months," Levi said. "And out of that span of time, how long have we been best friends?"

"One year, maybe?"

"I think it's one year and a half."

"Thereabouts." Maggie didn't want to argue with him that he had missed four months because he might accidentally bring up his ex-girlfriend. Maggie didn't have to argue with him about it. Levi had been single for one year and ten months. In that span of time, he and Maggie became best friends.

Levi's pop quiz wasn't over yet. "How long have we been dating?"

"Eight days. Why are you asking me all these questions, Levi?"

"What? Only eight days? It feels longer."

"You first held my hand fifteen days ago," Maggie reminded him.

"I was going to tell you that taking the next step forward is only natural, right?" Levi placed both hands on her shoulders.

"What next step, Levi?"

He looked shy all of a sudden. This was a first. Levi Theroux had never been shy.

"I've prayed about this all night."

Maggie lifted up her eyes to check his face. "You don't look tired."

"I fell asleep sometime in the middle of the night, but I assure you, when I got up this morning, I continued praying."

"About what exactly?"

"You and me and our future together."

Maggie liked his thoughtful tone. "Strategic planning."

"How long do you think we'll be together?" Levi asked.

"As long as God wants us to be?" Maggie chose a safe answer.

"What if He wants us to be together for a lifetime?"

"Then so be it."

"I like that answer." His eyelids dropped and so did his chin. Gently, he brushed his lips against

Maggie's jawline. He raised his chin and his lips gently teased hers.

Maggie giggled.

Levi quietened her with a soft caress as their lips found each other.

Around them, the morning sun shone, warming their hearts in the midwinter.

As slowly as he had begun, Levi lifted his lips away from hers. "Maggie."

"Yes?"

"Will you marry me?" His voice was quiet and pleasant. Undemanding. It sounded like one of their many conversations over casual things—

Wait a second.

"What?" Maggie pulled back in disbelief.

"You heard me."

"So soon?"

Levi held her hands. "Is it? We've just gone through our timeline. We've known each other for three years. A bunch of people have married after they've only known each other for three weeks or three months. Compared to their timeframes, three years sound like a very long time."

Maggie was stunned.

Levi was about to kneel down. Maggie stopped him. Levi looked disappointed.

"I'm not looking for a short-term relationship. As soon as we dated, I knew right away that you're the only one for me for the rest of my life. I've prayed about it and have peace about this. I'm confident that God has brought you to me. I'm sorry it took me more than a year to realize it." Levi's left hand was still in his jean pocket.

Maggie didn't want to think about what little shiny thing could be in that pocket.

"I know, but we've only dated for nine days," Maggie reminded him. "How about you ask me again in six months?"

"Six months?" Levi's left hand came out of his pocket empty-handed.

Maggie nodded.

"Then you'll give me an answer?"

"I will."

"You promise?" Levi's earnest face melted Maggie's heart.

She loved this man so much. "Okay. I promise."

"You need to make good on your promise." Levi went to his winter jacket that he had placed on a kitchen chair, and pulled out a blue gift box from one of its pockets.

He lifted up Maggie's hand and placed the box in her palm.

Maggie's heart thumped in her chest. She had seen this gift box before, but only one time when Tally's husband had given her a birthday present.

"Open it." Levi waited.

Maggie sat down on the lone armchair in the living room. She removed the white satin ribbon oh so carefully, and opened the box oh so slowly.

Inside were a pair of rings. Both identical except that one was bigger than the other.

They looked like platinum or white gold. The design included what looked like a cross, but it turned out to be a 'T' with a row of diamonds on one side.

"You promised to give me an answer in six months, so here are our promise rings." Levi knelt on the floor, and took the smaller ring out of the box.

"You came prepared with your Plan B." Maggie resisted asking how much those rings cost. "Is this yet another Christmas present from you?"

"You know me. Never let an opportunity slip by. I don't want to lose you, Maggie."

"If God wants us to be together, we'll be together. Ring or no ring."

"I know, but would you be willing to wear these couple's rings?" When Maggie looked stunned, Levi continued speaking. "If you don't like these, we can go back to Tiffany's together and get something you like."

"They're beautiful. I would've picked this ring myself."

Levi's face changed from nervous to relieved. "Since a wedding ring goes on the left ring finger, how about we wear our couple's promise rings on our right ring finger?"

Maggie lifted her right hand.

Levi slid the promise ring onto Maggie's right ring finger. "Looks a bit loose. We'll get it adjusted."

He handed his ring to Maggie. She put it on his right ring finger. Of course, it fit perfectly. "How did you decide on these rings?"

"I bought them a couple of days after we discussed buying this house," Levi explained. "At first, I thought we should go together to Phipps Plaza, but I didn't want to put you on the spot. Then I thought I could give it to you as a Christmas present. You could say no."

"I love it." Maggie lifted her right hand in the sun that had risen further in the sky, shining through the windows and spotlighting the sparkle in the ring.

She rested her head on Levi's shoulder. He wrapped his arms around her. They said nothing for a while.

Maggie felt bad that Levi had bought her all these things for Christmas. Her hand absentmindedly caressed his chin, where he'd trimmed his beard neatly, a contrast to his mop of curly hair.

With her own hair straight as a fiddle, she wondered what kind of hair their kids would inherit...

She sniffled a little.

Levi looked into her eyes. "Did I do something wrong?"

"What do you mean?"

"Did I surprise you too much today?"

Maggie shook her head. "Just felt a little lopsided, is all. You brought me a tabletop Christmas tree for this empty house, you baked me cookies to take to the Christmas luncheon, you donated two thousand dollars to missions, and now you bought these expensive couple's rings."

"Actually I forgot the jar of peaches I wanted to get for you from the Village bazaar."

"I love those. I can buy them myself next week. The Christmas Village goes on until January."

"Maybe they should have a permanent store, you know, that sells souvenirs and craft products year round. Some sort of a general store," Levi said.

"Good idea. I'll mention that to Bina the next time I see her. Will credit you, of course, for the idea."

Levi kissed Maggie's forehead.

"Anyway, my point is that you gave me so

much for Christmas, but all I got for you was a gift card." She pointed to the card that was still on the breakfast counter.

She could say that her excuse was that she had to pack up forty years of Jacobs family possessions in this house and had no time to shop for presents. The only thing she had done was to buy a knitted crossbody bag for Mom. As for Dad and Malachi, they were both getting gift cards.

"You chose me." Levi held Maggie's hands. "That's the best Christmas present you can give me. It's priceless. I ask for nothing else."

"You chose me too." Maggie's voice was quiet.

She hadn't expected Levi to reciprocate her love at all, so she was only prepared to be alone this Christmas—which was supposed to be her last one in Atlanta.

Now everything was different.

God had dramatically changed the direction of her life, and she was back to where she had started: Atlanta. All her plans for moving out of state and starting over had gone out the window.

Yet it felt like she was starting anew. God's better plan for her career and ministry would be more suitable for her skillset. And His choice of man for her was the one she had secretly loved for a year.

What more could she ask for?

Chapter Nineteen

"My first month of work at Midtown Village was easy because you've worked hard since July to make the Christmas Village run like clockwork." Erika's voice sounded like she was longing for December again.

Maggie listened as she drove the van from Midtown Chapel to the Midtown Warehouse.

Tally used to drive this van, shuttling among three places: church, the Village, and the warehouse. While Maggie missed Tally, her capacity for work, and her steady energy, she did not miss the work itself as a ministry assistant. Been there, done that.

It had been three months after Christmas, and

the trees and bushes along the road were starting to bud. Spring was here, and March called for short sleeves and preparation for Easter in three days. This year, Easter would fall on the first day of April. Maggie preferred to call it Resurrection Sunday, since that was the day Christians commemorated the resurrection of Jesus Christ from the grave, after His epic sacrifice on the cross for the sins of the world.

"To God be the ultimate glory," Maggie said.

In the passenger seat, Erika nodded.

"Teamwork," Maggie added. "In a church this size, and in the non-profit ministry that is Midtown Village, nothing happens without teamwork."

Maggie pointed out small bursts of azaleas along the side of the streets. "Sometimes they don't bloom until April, but nice to see the colors early before Easter Sunday."

"They are pretty. In Key Largo, you don't see these types of flowers."

"Mostly coconut trees and palm?"

"Pretty much. It's subtropical and all."

"Bet you get the ocean breeze and it's lovely like that."

"Sunrise on the beach…" Erika looked into the distance. "Before I moved to Atlanta, I attended a very small church that meets by the ocean. We call it the outdoor church because our church services are always outdoors by the ocean unless it's raining."

"Is Outdoor Church the name of your church?" Maggie asked.

"No, it's actually Beach Town Church. Pastor Butler is really nice. His wife, Chiyoko, led my mom and me to Christ three years ago."

"Praise the Lord that your church is doing Gospel work. Now you have a church to attend in the city and a church to go home to on the beach."

"I would've missed my old church more, but Mom's here with me now, so I don't have a reason to drive all the way to Key Largo."

"That's nice that she decided to move here rather than elsewhere." Maggie flicked on the turn signal at the stop sign.

"She wouldn't have if she hadn't broken up with her boyfriend. He was going to marry her, but things didn't work out." Erika turned to Maggie. "Why can't things work out nicely all the time?"

"Wouldn't that be great?"

Erika sighed. "I'm just glad that working at a church ministry is fun, and at least that's a relief from my otherwise blah day listening to Mom complain all the time about her 'sorry life,' you know?"

Fun? Shall I tell her the truth now? Burst the bubble three months in?

Maggie stopped at a red light. "It's not always fun, so cherish the moment."

"Not always fun?" Erika sounded surprised.

"Hate to break it to you that you're new to church work and you're in your honeymoon period."

"So I haven't seen reality?"

Maggie kept the speed limit. "You are seeing some of the reality. I love my work at church. I do consider it fun and fulfilling. However, I remind myself that it's not always fun and games. There are dark moments and you have to go through valleys of the shadow of death."

"Sounds scary."

"I don't mean to scare you. It's a reality check if you want to continue to work at Midtown Chapel. I can't speak for any other church, but our church is big. Along with the size comes challenges."

"Why, though?"

"You probably know the answer. A biblical church of Jesus Christ is always at the frontline of spiritual warfare, so you'll have to soldier on when things get tough," Maggie explained. "Be all read-up in your daily Bible devotional. Wear the full armor of God. Walk with God. Then you're ready to face the ups and downs of church life—and you have to do it by the power of the Holy Spirit."

"And only in."

"Yes. You got it." Maggie nodded. "If you fight a spiritual battle with your flesh, you lose. Only in the power of God can you survive."

"Wow, Maggie."

Maggie slowed down the van behind rush-hour traffic, which had already begun. It was nearly four o'clock in the afternoon. Metro Atlanta rush hour could go on for a while. Back in the old days, they used to taper off around six o'clock, but these days, it would not be surprising to see traffic jams at seven o'clock.

"Tell me more, Maggie." Erika turned to look at Maggie.

Maggie kept her eyes on the road. "Don't get me wrong. When you watch a pastor at the pulpit on TV, you don't see all the church dynamics and spiritual battles that go on behind close doors."

"I've started to notice that when I came here. It looks great on TV, but then behind the scene, they had to make sure the livestream works, the internet is not cut off, and so forth."

"Right. And in the sanctuary itself, the microphones better be working so that the preacher is not interrupted. If the sound system is broken, Pastor Kim's soft-spoken voice can't carry all the way to the second floor balcony, let alone be broadcast on the internet."

"Much prayer required," Erika said.

"For sure. Also, did you notice all the security personnel all around the building on Sunday mornings? A few years ago, a deranged person entered the building in the middle of the church service and threatened to shoot everyone if the pastor could not guarantee his ticket to heaven."

"Only God can guarantee your ticket to heaven and that ticket's name is Jesus Christ."

"We know that, but does the world know that?"

"I see now the warfare going on between good and evil, and the church is the battleground."

"Truth be told, Christians just want to worship God in peace. It's our right as a free country to have freedom of religion. Along with freedom comes a price."

"The price tag of security."

"Well, we also have many families in church, and therefore, many children in the nursery and preschool all the way to elementary and high school. We need the security teams to protect our children as well so that parents feel safe when they are in church—especially in downtown Atlanta, you know—even though this midtown area is just outside the center of the city, so we're between downtown and Buckhead."

"Crime is everywhere."

"Exactly." Maggie pulled onto the road that led to the church warehouse. Clouds had moved in and she wondered if it was going to rain later on.

"Sometimes Christians can have a rosy view of the pastor and his congregation. Many times I've heard people say, 'Oh wow! You attend Midtown Chapel? What is it like to be right in front of Pastor Kim and hear him preach live?' Funny thing is, Pastor Kim probably can't see us in the sanctuary because the lights are on him all the time."

Erika laughed. "Like he's some celebrity." Erika laughed. "My mom asked me that. She's been telling everyone that I work for Pastor Kim. I mean I haven't spoken with Pastor Kim since I started work. I'm just the admin assistant of the Midtown Village, which is now its own non-profit organization, independent from the church. Even though we still work together to organize events, you're not involved in my admin work and I'm not involved in yours."

"Right. But outsiders might not understand." Maggie pulled into the warehouse parking lot. She went around the building toward the loading dock at the back of the warehouse. "I can say two things about that. Firstly, never elevate a pastor to the level of a deity."

"I hear you. Sometimes people worship a pastor of a church instead of God. They ask 'What would pastor so-and-so do in this situation?' rather than pray about what Jesus would do."

"Not just 'they' who are out there somewhere, but I have to remind myself—as a staff member of the church—that I must never forget that Pastor Kim is only human, with his own sins and frailties and weaknesses and problems and so forth."

"Therein is the spiritual battle that you spoke of earlier."

"Yes. Every church, big or small, has its challenges and battles, but you knew that."

"I know that now."

"Secondly, about what you said earlier, you are not 'just the admin assistant,' Erika. As a believer of Christ, you are, first and foremost, a child of God, an ambassador of the King of Kings, a servant of the Lord of Lords."

"Good reminder."

"For me as well. Thing is, because we work in

a church, our burden is heavier, you know? It doesn't mean we lie about our lives. I get tired. I get upset. Sometimes my spirit is willing but my body is weak. I think as an example to others, we have to be authentic in our walk with the Lord. Be honest about our own mistakes and errors. Be willing to grow in the Lord. Let God make us more spiritually mature."

"I have a long way to go."

"Same here. I told you about my detour to Florida and back. I could have left town and gone to Lakeside—as wonderful as that place is—and missed God's perfect will for my life, which includes a job that matches my skillset and a boyfriend who loves me. I'd miss out on God's best if I go off on my own. All that to say that as a Christian, I'm not afraid to say, 'I messed up.' And I'm not afraid to learn."

"Thank you for that. I feel like I have to be on top of things at the Midtown Village, and it's a lot of pressure."

Maggie recalled training Erika for over a month back in November and December. Hadn't that been enough?

"I'm a phone call away, and you can come see me in my office. Just let Lindsay know, and she'll pencil you into a spot on my calendar. We can also have lunch and you can text me. If

I'm not in a meeting, I will reply to your messages."

"Thank you so much, Maggie."

"I've been busy the last three months getting organized in my new job, but things are settling down a bit, so come see me. How about we have lunch every Friday at church and we can talk about our week?"

"I'd like that," Erika said.

Maggie reversed the van so that the back cargo door faced the loading dock. The boxes they were transporting were probably not too heavy but they would fill the van. So the closer she could get to the loading dock, the better.

She had done this so many times that it was easy for her. She put the van in park and turned off the ignition.

Erika blinked and her lips quivered. Tears flowed from her eyes.

"Hey." Maggie was stunned. Erika had looked so cheerful just now that it was hard to see something else bubbling underneath. Was it the pressure of work?

Erika had brought her own tissue in her purse. She wiped her eyes. "I lied."

"We can talk."

"Don't we have to go inside and get those boxes for the kitchen?"

"They can wait. Talk to me. I'm listening."

"I lied. I'm not having fun. I'm having a terrible time." Erika sniffled. "My manager is also new here, and she is still adjusting to the environment. Since we're both new, it's like we're both having to learn together. She wants to look good in front of Mrs. Kim and Hiroki and the vendors and everyone else, but I'm having to cover for her every single day."

Maggie nodded.

Wait. Hiroki?

Since when had Hiroki Yamada and Erika started on a first-name basis?

"I shouldn't say anything bad about my boss, but…" Erika drew a deep breath. "I felt like quitting because I can't… I mean she called me at ten o'clock at night, asking for a report that she forgot to tell me about, and she told me I should have been independent enough to get it done before she asked. That's not reasonable."

No. It isn't.

Maggie didn't want to say it aloud because she didn't know Erika well enough to know whether she would then blurt out to Bina Marley that the Women's Event Coordinator had called the director "unreasonable." Maggie had worked long enough in this big church to be aware about interdepartmental politics.

At the same time, she wanted to minister to Erika.

Lord, show me what I need to say to her.

"I stayed up all night, did my best with the time I had, and came up with a report that I thought she wanted. The next day, it turned out to be the wrong report, and she blamed me for it in front of everyone, including RYUCP."

"By RYUCP, you mean Hiroki."

Erika nodded. "And his assistant, Alden."

Maggie didn't want to comment on Bina's modus operandi after work hours. In a non-profit ministry that depended on charitable donations, how could Erika ask for overtime pay if she ended up working all night on a last-minute report?

Maggie didn't know whether Bina had forgotten about the report or what. Besides, the Village was no longer her concern—except for collaborative projects between the church and its non-profit entity.

"Who asked Bina for the report in the first place?" Maggie asked. "Was it Hiroki?"

Erika nodded again. "It's for the new land, not the Village."

"That's a very big project. Bigger than the Village. I'm sorry you're the admin assistant now because it's a lot of pressure on you if you're new to this."

"I'm super stressed out. I had like maybe three hours of sleep the last few nights running around in circles for my boss."

Was Erika burning out already?

"Want to know what I used to do when Tally and I were involved in the Village?" Maggie said.

"Tell me."

"Whenever Hiroki asked Tally for a report on the tiny homes, I called or texted Alden to give me the specifics. I wanted to know precisely what Hiroki wanted. Alden would verify it for me. He's Hiroki's assistant to this day—and your peer—and he's very good at his job. You need to have his phone number on speed dial. You won't miss a single report this way."

"Okay. I forgot about Alden. He told me he gets off work at six o'clock. So I don't call his office after five just in case he's gone early, you know. But my boss would text me after hours asking for this and that, and I cannot ignore her. It feels as though she considers it taken care of if she just sends me a text, and I'm scrambling all night while she gets her beauty sleep." The tears flowed again.

Poor thing.

All this time, Erika didn't mention Bina Marley by name. She must be really hurt by her seemingly disorganized boss who had publicly shamed her for a report that could have been better handled.

How can I advise her about this without getting involved?

Getting involved meant she could talk to Mrs. Kim about it, who would then confront Bina for overworking her assistant. Or she could call Hiroki…or Alden.

Alden took Maggie's call at any time of day or night, but it might not apply to everyone. Also, he'd given her his personal number, which Maggie had no permission to share with Erika.

"Have you had any meeting with Alden, just the two of you?" Maggie asked.

"No. Why would I?"

"You're both working on the tiny homes. He assists Hiroki. You assist Bina. It makes sense for you and Alden to talk and come up with a system. He might give you an overview of all the reports that Hiroki often asks for whenever it comes to these projects. Hiroki is focused on ROIs. If the return on investment is low, it's a problem for him. After all, he is a partner in RYUCP, and that company is heavily invested in Midtown Village and the adjacent property."

"I see. I should call Alden and get on the same page with him."

"Call Alden tomorrow—no, wait. Tomorrow

is Good Friday, so maybe wait until next week when our church staff lunchroom is open again. I was going to suggest that you ask for a lunch meeting with Alden. He'll have to pay for lunch since he's not a church staff."

"I can pay for him."

"We used to give out guest coupons for lunches, but times are tough."

"I know. Besides, it's eight dollars, so anyone can pay."

"They should raise it to ten dollars since it's a full meal with appetizers, salad, main meal, and dessert, plus ice cream, but nobody asked me." Maggie waited to see if Erika had anything else she wanted to say.

"Well. I feel better now."

"Let's pray and ask God to give you wisdom and strength."

Erika lowered her head and closed her eyes, as though waiting for Maggie to pray. So she did.

"Lord Jesus, we come before You with a heavy burden in our hearts. Your Bible reminds us that Your burden is easy and light. We surrender this burden to You," Maggie prayed. "Lord, please show my sister in Christ, Erika, why You have allowed her to be here at this time. Perhaps she is the only one who can do this job right now. For such a time as this, there is no one else better than

Erika in this job as administrative assistant at Midtown Village. I pray that You will show her how to use all that she already knows from her marketing degree from college and her prior experience as an assistant manager in Key Largo, and show her great and mighty things she doesn't know—as mentioned in Jeremiah 33:3—about the uniqueness of ministry work."

Maggie paused to see if Erika wanted to pray. She did not. So Maggie continued.

"Lord Jesus, remind us of Your calling for our career and life. Ultimately, may Your perfect will prevail at Midtown Chapel, Midtown Village, and also RYUCP. Give us mercy and grace every day as we labor for You, Lord. It's very hard work, but nothing is harder than when You had to sacrifice Your life on the cross to rescue us from our sins. I pray these in Your strong and holy name. Amen."

"Amen." Erika looked up. "It's hard."

"I know. Trust me, I know. My first year as an admin assistant was crazy. I carried around a resignation letter in case I needed to drop it on Tally's desk," Maggie recalled. "Tally was an excellent boss—and she has now become my friend—but I tell you, the workload was overwhelming and I was so stressed out that I thought my hair was falling out. And I was only twenty-four years old."

"That bad, huh."

"Yeah. Then one day the Lord gave me an anchor verse that defined my new mindset to the whole pressure cooker. Matthew 5:16."

Let your light so shine before men, that they may see your good works and glorify your Father in heaven.

"That means that all that I do, I do for the Lord. I do my best for the Lord, and my best needs to shine. No matter what the circumstances are, I have to glorify the Lord," Maggie said. "Since I'm shining for the Lord, He will be my deliverer. If I am maligned, I look to the Lord. If I am defamed, I look to the Lord. If I am in the wrong, I ask God to forgive me and I correct it as soon as possible."

"You sound like you speak from experience."

Maggie chuckled. "I don't know how many times I've said sorry to Tally because I messed up or didn't understand the vendors we dealt with or something or other. Then she helped me clean up the mess. Over time, I got better as her assistant and then our ministry flourished, to the glory of God."

Maggie missed Tally. Some people had told Maggie that it was rare for a former boss to become a good friend. In many ways, Tally was more like an older sister whom Maggie never had.

"Tally often reminded me not to take things personally. It took me a while to get it, but I finally learned. When I have work issues, that's a work problem, not a personal attack on my personhood, you know? I have to look at it objectively so that I don't take everything personally, internalize the chaos, and crumble under pressure. You should see the Bible verses I taped everywhere to remind me to pray, pray, pray."

Erika wiped her eyes and stopped crying. "I need an anchor verse. One or more."

"Remember what I said earlier, that as a church worker, I must read my Bible and pray and wear the full armor of God? Ephesians 6:10-13 clearly outlined preparation for spiritual battles."

Finally, my brethren, be strong in the Lord and in the power of His might. Put on the whole armor of God, that you may be able to stand against the wiles of the devil. For we do not wrestle against flesh and blood, but against principalities, against powers, against the rulers of the darkness of this age, against spiritual hosts of wickedness in the heavenly places. Therefore take up the whole armor of God, that you may be able to withstand in the evil day, and having done all, to stand.

"Did you even think the battle would be inside a church or a ministry?"

Erika shook her head.

"Neither did I when I first started working in a church. Sometimes the hardest people to deal with are other Christians," Maggie said. "Ephesians 6:14-18 reminded me that I need God's protection at all times, whether inside the church or outside the church. In this world, really."

Stand therefore, having girded your waist with truth, having put on the breastplate of righteousness, and having shod your feet with the preparation of the gospel of peace; above all, taking the shield of faith with which you will be able to quench all the fiery darts of the wicked one. And take the helmet of salvation, and the sword of the Spirit, which is the word of God; praying always with all prayer and supplication in the Spirit, being watchful to this end with all perseverance and supplication for all the saints.

Maggie could feel the sun moving in the sky. How long had they been sitting in the van? She glanced at the dashboard clock. It was 5:35 p.m. Still, she didn't consider it to be a waste of time. She knew that Erika needed this moment.

"I guess we better go get the boxes before the warehouse closes at six." Maggie reached between the seats for her crossbody bag that contained her phone, tablet, and a slim credit card wallet.

It was the same teal bag that Levi had bought for her at the Christmas bazaar back in December. She had found this bag convenient and handy to carry around her whenever she went to meetings at or away from church.

Mom had the same bag, except hers was tangerine in color. Mom loved it too and carried it with her everywhere as well.

When she turned back to face the steering wheel, she was startled by a knock on her driver's side window.

Levi stood there, a look of concern on his face. He was wearing a polo shirt with the church logo embroidered on it.

On the passenger side, Erika opened her door. "I'll go sign out the boxes. You talk to your boyfriend. Thanks for driving the van here with me."

"I'll wait for you. Take your time. No worries." Maggie smiled.

Maggie opened her driver's side door and stepped out.

"How did you end up driving the van?" Levi reached for Maggie's right hand. He touched her promise ring.

"They need to move some boxes from here to

the Village, and I happen to have a meeting there today, so I volunteered to drive the church van so they can use it to haul the boxes."

"Where did you park your car?"

"At church."

"So you have to drive back there to get your car." He checked the clock on his phone. "It will be late before we have dinner."

"It'll be all right," Maggie assured him. She'd explain to him later, but this wasn't the time.

"Why don't you let Erika drive the van back to the Village and then she can figure out how to get it to church? You can carpool with me home to your house for our dinner. Tomorrow morning I'll pick you up and take you to church."

Maggie studied his face. "Isn't that a lot of trouble for you?"

"Not when I'm with you. I was trying to find ways to be with you."

"Wait." Maggie laughed. "Church is closed tomorrow, Levi. It's Good Friday. Did you forget?"

"Ah, I sure did."

"How about this? I drive the van to the Village and drop off the boxes. Then I drive back to church and pick up my car. I can meet you at the house." It was what Maggie had planned in the first place.

"That's a lot of time away from you."

"Or you can always follow me to the Village and church, and we can caravan to my house." Well, she said "my house" but it was currently only a rental. Mom and Dad had agreed to rent the house to her until she and Levi could afford to buy it from them.

"I suppose I can do that. Then we will have both vehicles." Levi frowned a bit. "I was hoping to drive with you."

"I see. We've only dated for three months and you're clingy already."

Levi gently pulled Maggie toward him. He leaned against her face. "This is the halfway point. Three more months and I get to ask you again."

Maggie knew exactly what he meant. In retrospect, she could have said yes back in December, and they'd be engaged already. However, she wanted them to make sure that they were doing the right thing in the perfect will of God.

So, they had to wait.

His breath was warm against her ears. He planted a quick kiss on her cheek.

Maggie stepped back. "The camera's on!"

"Why can't I show my affection to my future wife?" He lifted her right hand and his right hand in the direction of the cameras that were mounted on the outside wall of the building somewhere.

My future wife.

Maggie didn't protest.

"Besides, today is my last day here, remember? Monday I'll be starting my new job at Christmastown."

"How does your last day feel, Mr. Theroux?"

"Just as I told Pastor Kim last week, I maxed out all my potential here. Time for me to utilize my BBA."

Maggie agreed that he should put his Bachelor of Business Administration and ten years of experience in the industry to good use. "And you thought Christmastown just wanted you to be the warehouse manager over there."

"Isn't it amazing how God works?"

"Yeah."

Back in December, the warehouse manager position had been the only job that Christmastown had offered him, but Levi explained to them that he might as well stay at the church warehouse if he were doing the same thing elsewhere.

Two months later, God worked it out because the man slated for the regional director position, Rasheed Bolton, decided to retire from work altogether so that he could spend more time with his grandchildren. Cyrus then offered Levi a chance to interview for the vacant position. Out of thirty-nine candidates, Levi rose to the top.

Starting on the Monday after Easter Sunday,

Levi would be the new regional director of Christmastown Atlanta.

"I'm so proud of you," Maggie said. "Praise the Lord for how He has worked in our lives."

"Praise the Lord indeed."

Chapter Twenty

$\mathcal{I}$t had been seven months to the day since Levi proposed and Maggie told him to ask her again in six months.

Now he was one month late.

Maggie began to second guess her judgment on Christmas Day. Therein was the catch. She felt that if they were engaged on Christmas Day, it would affect the real meaning of Christmas.

It would be better for them to have a day of their own.

She had been waiting for that day ever since.

Winter had given way to spring and now it was July, arguably one of the hottest months of the summer—the other being August.

The Midtown Moms conference went all day

today—and would be all week—keeping Maggie busy at the Midtown Village community center.

It was almost five o'clock, and the conference was wrapping up on the first day.

Sixteenth of July on a Monday was ending, and still, there was no text or phone call from Levi today.

At all.

Had he forgotten that it was exactly seven months today?

Maybe he was busy.

That could be said for both of them. Maggie had been busy for the last few weeks, preparing for today's conference kick-off.

Perhaps Levi was even busier at Christmas-town as their new regional director, replacing his retired predecessor. The surprise turn of events was a godsend for Levi's career.

Levi had enjoyed his work there, but since they had bought a new warehouse in Duluth in metro Atlanta, Maggie was only able to see him after work hours.

She missed him during the day. Gone were the days when he'd show up unannounced in her office to drink her coffee or she'd go to the church warehouse and he'd help her get whatever she needed for the Village.

Today was such a day when she missed him.

Oh, what am I doing?

Sitting at the back table, the one nearest to the kitchen door, Maggie took a deep breath. She wanted to pray, but she didn't want to close her eyes just in case the speaker thought she had fallen asleep.

Forgive me, Lord, for losing my focus.

An oft-quoted passage of Scripture popped into her head. She had read Philippians 4:6-7 during her morning devotionals. Her parents had mentioned it. Dad had preached on it. And so had Pastor Kim.

Today, Maggie needed the reminder.

Be anxious for nothing, but in everything by prayer and supplication, with thanksgiving, let your requests be made known to God; and the peace of God, which surpasses all understanding, will guard your hearts and minds through Christ Jesus.

Why was she anxious? She had no idea.

The afternoon session was over now, and the speaker prayed to close out the first day's activities. It was a heartfelt prayer with many echoes of "amens" from the attendees.

Then Maggie went up to the microphone to remind the ladies to leave their name tags at the check-in table so that they would have them the next day.

"You have half an hour to pick up your children from childcare," Maggie added. "I'll be around here for a few minutes and then I'm going to leave. I don't know about you all, but it's been a long day."

A number of moms agreed with her.

"Take it easy tonight and come back refreshed tomorrow. We're going to have some interesting fun in the morning. Wear comfortable clothes and be prepared to sit on the floor. Bring floor cushions if you want."

Maggie waved to her crew, signaling that they could start taking down the round tables. In the morning, the activities would be different than today's. There would be skits and drama that perhaps some of the mothers who had theater background would appreciate.

She went back to her table at the back and packed up her stuff. She put her tablet and phone into the knitted crossbody bag, and carried the binder in her hand.

The community center door opened to a hallway with ceiling fans. Even so, there was a big contrast between the air conditioned room inside and the furnace out there that was July in Atlanta.

Of course, Atlanta was not as hot as Lakeside,

Florida, in the summer, but it could get pretty hot, even for a native resident like Maggie. No wonder people sometimes called this city Hotlanta.

Maggie stepped outside into the high humidity. She started to sweat but it wasn't too bad because she wore a cotton blouse and skirt.

She had forgotten her sunglasses. She'd left them in her office at Midtown Chapel. So she placed a hand on her temple to act as a temporary visor as she walked across the grassy Village square to get to the parking lot.

A shadow moved in front of her.

"Oh good. Cloud cover."

Nope. Not cloud cover. Too low for it.

She squinted in the afternoon light. And looked again.

It was Levi. "Hey sweetheart."

"Whatcha doing here? Did you get off work early?" Maggie was genuinely surprised to see Levi. Usually they'd meet at the house and do some more cleaning or painting.

"Don't worry. I drove safely." A small blue velvet box appeared in his hand.

As if on cue, the sun moved behind a puffy cloud.

And Levi went down on his knees.

Maggie's heart skipped a beat.

Breathe. Breathe.

Maggie had waited seven months for this, but she still found herself in disbelief. She stared at Levi, wondering what he was up to.

A crowd gathered around them, waiting.

"Maggie, on Christmas Day seven months ago, I proposed to you," Levi said. "You said to ask you again six months later. Sorry I'm late, but I was preparing a gift for you that couldn't be ready until this week."

Did he mean the gift in his hands right now?

He opened the velvet box and lifted it up for Maggie to see. The princess cut diamond sparkled in the sun.

"I love you, Maggie," Levi said. "I love your steadiness and your desire to be in God's will for your life. I love your kind heart, your sweet disposition, all of you. I love everything about you, my best friend on earth."

Maggie tried not to lose it. "I love you too, Levi. You were there when I was sick. Took care of me, took me to the doctor, made me chicken soup. You always make sure I lack nothing, that I'm comfortable. With you, I feel safe and secure. God has given you to me."

Sweat trickled down Levi's forehead. He soldiered on. "Remember what I said after the Christmas Eve service?"

"Yes. Let's serve God together."

"Now I say let's serve God together as husband and wife, and in the future, with our children as well."

Maggie nodded. "We will raise them with the love of Christ and prayerfully our family will continue to serve God for generations to come."

Levi broke into a broad smile. "Magdalene Grace Jacobs, will you make me the happiest man alive by becoming my one and only wife? You're the only one for me."

It was so hot out that this man deserved an answer now.

Maggie smiled back to him, her answer at the ready. In fact, she'd been wanting to say yes since the day after Christmas. "Yes, Matthew Levi Theroux. I'll marry you."

The crowd around them broke out in applause. Residents of Midtown Village, members of Midtown Moms, church staff, Village leaders, and passers by all clapped and hollered.

Levi grinned as he placed the engagement ring on Maggie's left finger.

Camera shutters snapped, and Maggie was suddenly aware of photographers and videographers all around them.

Good thing I said yes.

She wondered how much Levi paid for them to be here to record this moment in time. Then she felt underdressed in her cotton attire and sandals. Oh well. At Midtown Chapel, she was used to cameras in the sanctuary, and cameras in the hallways, always filming this or that.

Maggie pulled Levi to his feet.

The photographers continued their work, capturing the moment when Levi drew Maggie into his embrace. They were both sweating in the sweltering heat, but they didn't care.

Levi had finally popped the question again. What were a few more minutes of sunshine?

Levi lifted Maggie's chin toward his and gave her a preview of what would come—a future husband's gentle kiss for his beloved future wife.

Chapter Twenty-One

*F*our months later, Levi stood in front of the full-length mirror in the men's choir changing room, and adjusted his bow tie. His best man and cousin, Cyrus, had left the room to check on his pregnant wife, Amy, who was their wedding photographer. She could have sent another photographer in her place, but she insisted on handling it herself.

The wedding ceremony would be in two hours, but Levi came to church at the same time as Maggie so that he could be in the same building with her. In case she needed something.

So far she hadn't called or checked on him. She had said she'd be busy in the women's choir changing room—which doubled up as the bridal room—on the other side of the sanctuary, getting her makeup done and so forth.

Her matron of honor, Tally Moss, was with her. She had flown all the way from the Bahamas to stay for several days to catch up with Maggie, to help her prepare for the wedding, and no doubt to see her sister Colette, the wedding planner, and the rest of the Fitzpatrick family.

Levi checked his hair in the mirror. He'd gotten a haircut the day before, but his usual hairdresser wasn't there, and his replacement didn't know how to handle curly hair and cut it too short. He wasn't used to it. "Oh well. It'll grow back."

He sat down on an armchair in the empty room next to the clothes rack where two rental tuxedo jackets hung on hangers, closed his eyes, and tried not to think of his bad haircut—only on the most important day in his and Maggie's life together.

Speaking of Maggie, Levi wondered how she was doing at that moment. He wanted to text her but he didn't want to get her all nervous.

At least they could all stay put in this building until the ceremony was over. Walking downstairs or taking the elevator down to the fellowship hall for the reception was easier than going outside in the cold and driving fifteen minutes to the

Midtown Village community center—which wasn't available anyway due to the Christmas Village being in full swing until January.

The fellowship hall at Midtown Chapel was also fully booked in December, and only available on the Saturday before Thanksgiving. And they had to reserve it months in advance or they'd lose it.

Levi had been disappointed that they couldn't have their wedding at church on the sixteenth of December, the one year anniversary of their first kiss on the Village square.

Did he want a wedding at their home church or not? They could always go to another venue outside the church, but as Midtown Chapel members, they didn't have to pay for the sanctuary or the fellowship hall.

"Therefore, we should be flexible about the date," Maggie had told him when they discussed the reservation problem.

Practical Maggie.

"To begin with, God is sovereign," she said, to which Levi agreed wholeheartedly. "The fellowship hall is free to Midtown members, thereby saving us a pretty penny. Moving the wedding forward means that when we honeymoon all week at Lakeside, we could spend Thanksgiving with my parents. My mom roasts the most delicious brined turkey."

And so that had been how their wedding date ended up being in November and not December.

Levi had left the logistics of their wedding to Maggie, and true to form, the event coordinator delegated the work to experts in the field. She hired wedding planner Colette Fitzpatrick from Lakeside Resort to organize their wedding, destination wedding photographer Amy Theroux to capture the event, and Chef Forsythia and the Village kitchen crew to make finger food for the reception.

Their budget wedding planned, Levi turned his attention to fixing up his townhouse, staging it, and putting it on the market. He moved most of his furniture into Maggie's house, which she was temporarily renting from her parents until they worked out the details of buying the house.

Since his inheritance money had paid for his townhouse, any sale would be pure profit. That, plus the remainder of his inheritance money could go toward buying the Jacobs' family home, leaving them with a small loan to get from the bank.

However, after taking a couple's financial course at church, and undergoing three months of rigorous premarital counseling, Levi and Maggie felt uneasy about starting their marriage saddled with debt. That would put a dark cloud over their honeymoon and marital bliss.

Therefore, no loans for them.

How could they buy the Jacobs' family home in Atlanta, then?

Maggie's parents asked them to name the price they could pay for the four-bedroom house. Levi and Maggie prayed about it, decided to set Maggie's savings aside and only used up Levi's inheritance money plus the sale of the townhouse.

Levi's townhouse sold quickly within a week of its listing. It sold for a good sum, being in a desirable neighborhood with houses more expensive than his. An investor with cash in hand bought the house. Levi would rather have sold it to a family where they could raise their children, instead of to an investor who had told them their plans to rent out the place.

In any case, his townhouse was sold at a profit, enabling Levi and Maggie to name the price they could afford to buy the Jacobs' family home, which was still two hundred thousand dollars short of the asking price, unfortunately.

Their real estate agent, Sally, made the offer, citing repairs that the 1950s house would require, including a future new roof replacement.

To their amazement, Maggie's parents accepted their offer, which was way below market value. Perhaps they realized that Levi and Maggie had a lot of expenses, including the wedding, and they were starting out on a new journey together and could use a boost.

Nonetheless, God had provided.

They hadn't needed to create an LLC or turn the house into an investment property because they decided to make it their own family home.

Levi knew that he and Maggie would have to work for some years to come so they could have savings again and the all-important emergency fund.

While Maggie continued to stay at her parents' house, paying rent, Levi had to find a place to stay for two months until their wedding.

At first he wanted to rent a tiny house or go to an extended stay hotel or rent an apartment month by month, but Alden stepped in and offered his guest room for free.

God had provided again!

Alden wasn't such a bad guy after all. He hadn't had a chance to go out with Maggie, except as a part of work, and that didn't count as a date. Levi wished him well and prayed that he would find his own happily-ever-after.

As for the renovation of the old house, Levi and Maggie prayed and reminded each other of Proverbs 24:27.

Prepare your outside work,
Make it fit for yourself in the field;
And afterward build your house.

They decided that it would be better to replenish their savings, which had now been diversified into real estate. For now, they could live in that old house if they made only a few updates. Fresh paint, new carpet, and new air conditioner and heater units. Maggie was a hard worker, and if she and Levi couldn't do it themselves, she knew how to find deals and workers who could do the work at a reasonable price.

Even though they splurged and replaced all the windows with energy efficient insulated windows to save electricity during the hot summer and cold winters, the total cost of the updates was less than the five Tiffany rings he had bought out of his inheritance money before the remainder of it went to the purchase of the house. However, the two couple's rings, two wedding bands, and Maggie's engagement ring were all worth it.

Levi was pleased that Maggie was practical and didn't spend more money than necessary. Levi knew that with her, he wouldn't go broke. She was becoming the Proverbs 31 woman that the Bible spoke about. Levi recalled verses 10-11 from one of Pastor Kim's sermons.

Who can find a virtuous wife?
  For her worth is far above rubies.
  The heart of her husband safely trusts her;
  So he will have no lack of gain.

At the church office, Maggie put all of herself into her job as the women's event coordinator, and everyone who'd worked with her only sang praises about her dedication to God's work and ministry.

Levi couldn't be prouder of her work ethic.

The door opened, making Levi open his eyes and look in that direction. Cyrus came in, looking spiffy in his white shirt and bow tie.

"Getting some rest, huh?" Cyrus asked.

Levi realized that he had somehow slid down the armchair, so he sat up straight. He checked his vest to make sure that it wasn't wrinkled in the front. The back, he could hide when he put on the jacket.

"Hey man, thank you again for the honeymoon package you gifted us," Levi said.

He couldn't remember how many times he'd thanked Cyrus, but he was truly grateful. Cyrus and Amy had bought them a honeymoon package at Lakeside Resort, where they would stay in one of the honeymoon suites, go to the spa, walk in the woods, canoe on the lake, and generally take it easy for a week.

"Don't mention it. You know that we suggested Hawaii, where it's really warm and Amy knows some deals, but you and Maggie chose Lakeside."

Levi nodded. "Yes, since next Thursday is Thanksgiving Day, we might as well honeymoon at Lakeside, where we can visit with Maggie's Mom and Dad for Thanksgiving."

"I'm all for family." Cyrus smiled. "You ready to go?"

"Is it time already?" Levi checked his phone. Twenty minutes to go before his alarm went off. He canceled the alarm.

"Better turn off your phone too," Cyrus said.

"Good reminder."

The two men put on their tuxedo jackets and checked each other's collars and sleeves.

"Looking good, Cousin." Cyrus gave him two thumbs up. "I believe you're marrying the right person."

"God protected me, didn't He?"

"He sure did."

Once upon a time, Levi had thought that Soline was the one.

She wasn't.

Then he thought that Forsythia was his ideal type.

She wasn't.

When Levi reached the end of his choices, he turned to God and he talked to his best friend.

And saw her.

Finally saw her for who she really was.

Maggie Jacobs.

She had been there all along, comforting him when he was heartbroken, cheering him on when he tried to bounce back, and caring for him unconditionally.

It had been four years since Levi had known Maggie, two years since they'd been best friends, nine months since they'd started dating, and a whole lifetime ahead of them to continue to be with each other.

My best friend. And today, my wife.

The only woman he wanted to spend the rest of his life with—to hold and cherish, to love and care for.

The future mother of all his children.

Levi and Cyrus stood outside the sanctuary door, the same door that the men's choir used to get to the choir loft.

From behind closed doors, Levi could hear the string quartet playing a medley of wedding selections. They were pleasant to hear and the music was lovely, but Levi started getting nervous.

I'm getting married today!

He took slow, deep breaths.

"I've done this, and it's going to be fine." Cyrus patted his shoulder. "Tell you what's hard. That first child. Now that made me more nervous. But after the second, and now the third, I can just say 'whatever' and take things in stride."

Levi barely heard him.

"God has given Maggie to you. Rejoice. Cherish her. Look forward to it."

Now Levi heard every word Cyrus just said.

"Thanks."

"Let's pray before we go in or you'll be a wreck." Cyrus bowed his head.

Levi prayed along, hearing only every other word. "Amen."

He drew a deep breath and closed his eyes.

Lord Jesus, forgive me. I can barely pray. I was okay in the changing room. I don't know what happened between then and now. Give me strength. Give me grace. Give me mercy. In Your holy name, I pray. Amen.

When he opened his eyes, Pastor Kim was standing next to him in a suit and carrying his Bible.

"You only need to do this one time," he said in his grandfatherly voice—even though Pastor Kim wasn't a grandfather.

Levi nodded. He was glad that Pastor Kim was officiating the wedding ceremony today. It could've been Maggie's father, Pastor Jacobs, but

Levi didn't need the pressure. It could also have been Byron Moss, who was the assistant pastor at Midtown Chapel for some years, but he and his family had moved to pastor a church in Florida, about three hours away from Lakeside Chapel. In fact, Levi should see Byron and his wife, Tina, in the sanctuary.

As the string quartet began playing "Jesu, Joy of Man's Desiring," it was the cue for Levi, his best man, and the pastor to enter the sanctuary.

Levi tried to smile. He looked around and spotted Byron and Tina. Byron nodded, and Levi gained some confidence, knowing he was among friends.

He looked around the pews to find familiar faces. Oh, there was Gus, sitting alone because his wife was the matron of honor this afternoon. After their wedding, Gus had whisked Tally away to the Bahamas, where Tally continued her ministry as a much sought-after speaker in women's conferences around the world.

All the church warehouse staff sat together and Levi waved to them. He missed them since he'd taken up the new job at Christmastown. They all understood why he decided to help his cousin with the new expansion. They told him that it was a good thing for Cyrus to trust his cousin. Some other families had a hard time working together.

Christmastown workers from their Atlanta warehouse were there too. Cyrus waved to his employees. The holiday decorating company wanted to open a branch office in a high-rise building in Buckhead, but Levi told Cyrus that since they were new in town, he felt that his office should be in the warehouse for now, until the company had a foothold in the metro Atlanta market.

After Christmastown had reached the southeast, then perhaps Cyrus could buy or build a building for his regional headquarters or something.

Cyrus liked Levi's idea to save cost.

Malachi was seated near his mother, and they were both surrounded by the Fitzpatrick family. They had saved space on the pew for the eldest daughter, Colette, the wedding planner. Pastor Fizz was sitting by his wife, and they were chatting with Mrs. Kim, who was there with her daughter Iseul, who was Maggie's age.

Before long, the quartet stopped playing.

Levi's heart skipped a beat.

Slowly, the cellist began to play the notes for "Canon in D," and the violins and violas joined in for a beautiful rendition of Johann Pachelbel's masterpiece.

This was Maggie's favorite wedding music,

and hearing it now, Levi's heart was touched, as the double doors at the back of the hundred-year-old sanctuary opened, revealing Levi's bride in a long-sleeve winter wedding dress made of white tulle and satin and sequins.

On the arm of her father, retired Pastor Jacobs, Maggie made her way toward Levi, as the wedding guests stood on their feet and clapped and cheered.

Here comes my bride, the love of my life.

Levi thanked God for the best decision he ever made—other than accepting Jesus Christ for the salvation of his soul.

This afternoon, the Saturday before Thanksgiving, eleven months after his first proposal, he was finally marrying Maggie, his best friend who loved him no matter what, with whom he could be himself, who would travel through life with him, and enjoy the blessings of God with him.

Maggie was the lifetime partner he had been longing for, that he had found in no one else—all forsaken for her and her alone.

As Maggie stepped closer, Levi could see the diamond cross pendant on her neckline. It had belonged to his mother, passed on to him after she died. Now he would give it to the love of his life.

Before he knew it, Maggie's dad had placed her gloved right hand on his left hand.

Levi glanced at Maggie. She was smiling sweetly, but her eyes were teary.

She mouthed "I love you," and it warmed Levi's heart.

This was their happiest day to date in their relationship and both of them were in tears.

Tears of joy, not of sorrow.

Tears of hope for tomorrow.

Tears of thankfulness that God had brought them together and kept them together.

"I love you too," Levi mouthed back to Maggie.

And they held hands for the rest of the wedding ceremony, and for the rest of their lives together as Mr. and Mrs. Levi and Maggie Theroux.

~

Dear Reader:

Thank you for reading *Let Me Hold You* (Midtown Christmas Book 1). I hope you enjoyed this novel. The next novel is *Let Me Adore You*, the story of assistant manager Erika Song and architect Hiroki Yamada. To be notified when *Let Me Adore You* is published, sign up for my newsletter.

Book News from Jan Thompson
JanThompson.com/newsletter

If you have read the books in my other series and collections, you might have found that some of the characters in *Let Me Hold You* sound familiar, and you would be right.

Levi and Maggie's wedding guests included Tina and Byron Moss, who had moved away before *Let Me Hold You* began. Their story is told in *Smile for Me* (Vacation Sweethearts Book 1).

Smile for Me (Vacation Sweethearts Book 1)
JanThompson.com/smile

Erika Song appeared briefly in the supporting cast of *Look for Me* (Vacation Sweethearts Book 4). More about her past will be in Erika's story, *Let Me Want You* (Midtown Christmas Book 2).

Look for Me (Vacation Sweethearts Book 4)
JanThompson.com/look

We first met Levi and Maggie in the supporting cast of Tally and Gus's story in *Pray for Me* (Vacation Sweethearts Book 5), which featured the Fitzpatrick family.

Pray for Me (Vacation Sweethearts Book 5)
JanThompson.com/pray

In *Let Me Hold You*, we also met Levi's cousin, Cyrus, the CEO of Christmastown. The story of how he met his wife, Amy, is told in *Wish You Joy* (Savannah Sweethearts Books 10).

Wish You Joy (Savannah Sweethearts Book 10)
JanThompson.com/wish

Happy reading!

Joyfully in Jesus,
Jan Thompson

Acknowledgments

Many thanks to my Georgia Press publishing team for keeping up with my writing schedule.

I appreciate my editors Lesley Ann McDaniel for copyediting and Kim Kemery for proofreading this novel.

A special thank you to my loyal readers who have been with me from the beginning. You've waited patiently for me to write my books, and you never let up over the years. May God bless you!

I am grateful to God for my family's encouragement for my writing career.

And I'll always remember my beloved mother and my late father for having instilled in me the love of reading and writing from a very early age. I miss my father here on earth, but my mother and I will see him again in heaven some bright day.

Most of all, I am eternally thankful to my Lord and Savior, Jesus Christ, who died on the cross to save me from my sins and rose again from the grave to give me eternal life. Without Him, I can write nothing (John 15:5).

Jan Thompson

John 3:16

Books by Jan Thompson

Contemporary Christian Coastal and Beach
Romance

Seaside Chapel (7 Books)
JanThompson.com/seaside
Savannah Sweethearts (12 Books)
JanThompson.com/savannah
Vacation Sweethearts (8 Books)
JanThompson.com/vacation

Contemporary Christian City Romance

Midtown Christmas (4 Books)
JanThompson.com/christmas

Christian Romantic Suspense

Protector Sweethearts (6 Books)
JanThompson.com/protector
Defender Sweethearts (6 Books)
JanThompson.com/defender

Near-Future Tehnothrillers with Christian
Romance

Binary Hackers (4 Books)
JanThompson.com/binary

Subscribe to Jan Thompson's mailing list:
JanThompson.com/newsletter

Seaside Chapel

Welcome to *USA Today* bestselling author Jan Thompson's Seaside Chapel Christian beach romance series. These novels are set on real-life St. Simon's Island, Georgia—a beach town where history is all around and the future is a moment away—and the neighboring fictitious Seaside Island, where the rich and famous live.

Savor the small-town atmosphere and the warm southern beaches of St. Simon's Island and the idyllic Golden Isles along the Atlantic Ocean. Enjoy the music of the orchestra and hymns of the church, and hang out with our Christian friends who attend Seaside Chapel, a little church by the sea known for its beach weddings and fair share of love and life.

As these Christians grow in their knowledge

and understanding of God, they are tested in their spiritual maturity, their love lives, and their relationships with others. Share their heartaches and healing, and cheer them on as they celebrate faith, family, and friends.

JanThompson.com/seaside

- Book 0 (Prequel): *His Surprise Proposal*
- Book 1: *His Longing Heart*
- Book 2: *His Wake-Up Call*
- Book 3: *His Morning Kiss*
- Book 4: *His Quiet Serenade*
- Book 5: *His Waiting Love*
- Book 6: *His Beach Retreat*

Savannah Sweethearts

Welcome to the new south! From *USA Today* bestselling author Jan Thompson come these clean and wholesome, sweet and inspirational Christian romances set on the romantic beaches of Tybee Island and in the coastal town of Savannah, Georgia. Meet a group of multiracial and multiethnic churchgoing Christians who love the Lord, work hard in their careers, and seek God's will for their love lives. Against a backdrop of ocean, sand, and sun, these inspirational romances showcase aspects of the human need for God and for one another. Have some tea, settle in a comfortable reading chair, and enjoy these sweet celebrations of faith, hope, and love in Jesus Christ.

JanThompson.com/savannah

- Book 1: *Ask You Later* (Artist Romance)
- Book 2: *Know You More* (Multiracial Romance)
- Book 3: *Tell You Soon* (Asian-American Romance with Suspense)
- Book 4: *Draw You Near* (International Romance)
- Book 5: *Cherish You So* (Wheelchair Billionaire Romance)
- Book 6: *Walk You There* (Old-Meets-New Tour Guide Romance)
- Book 7: *Love You Always* (Romance with Suspense)
- Book 8: *Kiss You Now* (Multiracial Romance)
- Book 9: *Find You Again* (Multiracial Romance)
- Book 10: *Wish You Joy* (Christmas-Themed Romance)
- Book 11: *Call You Home* (Deaf Chef Romance)
- Book 12: *Let You Go* (Asian-American Romance with Suspense)

Read *Ask You Later* (Book 1) for free:
JanThompson.com/ask-free

Vacation Sweethearts

Travel with our friends from Savannah, Georgia, to the coast and to the mountains. Cheer them on as they celebrate the immeasurable grace and undeserved mercy of God through Jesus Christ.

The Vacation Sweethearts novels are a spin-off of Jan's Savannah Sweethearts series, and fans will recognize familiar faces from Riverside Chapel, a church in the coastal city of Savannah, Georgia. In fact, we might even visit the beach town of Tybee Island from time to time to visit old friends and beloved families...

JanThompson.com/vacation

- Book 0 (Prequel): *Time for Me*
- Book 1: *Smile for Me* (Beach Romance in the Bahamas)
- Book 2: *Reach for Me* (Romance with Suspense in the Smoky Mountains)
- Book 3: *Wait for Me* (Romance with Suspense on a Cruise Ship)
- Book 4: *Look for Me* (Romance with Suspense in a Florida Beach Town)
- Book 5: *Pray for Me* (International Romance in the City of Atlanta)
- Book 6: *Care for Me* (Small Mountain Town Romance)
- Book 7: *Cheer for Me* (International Romance)

Read *Time for Me* (Prequel) for free:
JanThompson.com/time-free

Midtown Christmas

Big city romance, small town feel. Four Christian couples minister at Midtown Chapel in metro Atlanta, and Midtown Village, the community of tiny homes for needy families. From November to January every year, this place turns into a Christmas Village for a small-town feel right there in the metropolis of Atlanta, Georgia.

- Book 1: *Let Me Hold You* (Levi Theroux and Maggie Jacobs from *Pray for Me*)
- Book 2: *Let Me Adore You* (Erika Song from *Look for Me* and Hiroki Yamada from *Walk You There*)
- Book 3: *Let Me Honor You* (Forsythia McDevitt from *Call You Home* and Owen Grayson from *Find You Again*)

- Book 4: *Let Me Love You* (Leila Patel from *Find You Again*)

Protector Sweethearts

Private investigator Helen Hu and her associates specialize in searching for missing persons and hunting for lost treasures. Join them in their adventure suspense around the world in *USA Today* bestselling author Jan Thompson's Protector Sweethearts, a series of Christian Romantic Suspense with a side of mystery.

Protector Sweethearts is a spin-off of Savannah Sweethearts and Vacation Sweethearts.

JanThompson.com/protector

- Book 1: *Once a Thief*

- Book 2: *Once a Hero*
- Book 3: *Once a Spy*
- Book 4: *Twice a Fighter*
- Book 5: *Twice a Convict*
- Book 6: *Twice a Soldier*

Defender Sweethearts

Defender Sweethearts is a sister series to the Protector Sweethearts Christian romantic suspense collection. While the heroes in Protector Sweethearts search for lost treasures and lost people, the Defender Sweethearts novels focus on protecting the helpless and hopeless. The main characters in Defender Sweethearts come from the supporting cast in Protector Sweethearts.

JanThompson.com/defender

- Book 1: *Never a Traitor*
- Book 2: *Never a Hostage*

Binary Hackers

Like more suspense with your Christian romance? Like to read suspense thrillers? If you're looking for clean near-future romantic suspense without compromising the Christian faith, these books are for you.

From *USA Today* bestselling author Jan Thompson come these inspirational near-future cyberthrillers combining technothriller and romance, starting with Binary Hackers that feature computer specialists living at the edge of cyberspace, where they have to juggle being law-abiding truth-telling Christians while carrying out their assignments by any and all means possible.

The Binary Hackers series is set in the same story world as Jan's other books, and characters from the other series may make cameo appearances in this series and vice versa.

JanThompson.com/binary

- Book 1: *Zero Sum*
- Book 2: *Zero Day*
- Book 3: *Zero Base*
- Book 4: *Zero Trust*

About Jan Thompson

USA Today bestselling author Jan Thompson writes clean and wholesome contemporary Christian romance with elements of women's fiction, Christian romantic suspense with an air of mystery, and inspirational international thrillers with threads of sweet Christian romance. Jan's books are for readers who love inspiring stories of faith, family, and friends.

Raised on a tropical island in the eastern hemisphere, Jan now lives and writes in the western hemisphere. Her international background gives her a unique multicultural and multiracial perspective to her novels and books. The island has never left her, and she reminisces about beach life in her beach romance novels.

When Jan is not busy writing small-town stories, she writes big-city romantic suspense and international technothrillers, a nod to her previous career in computer science. She weaves technology with human interests, reflecting the current and future digital world. And romance. There's always romance.

Beyond the printed page, Jan is a wife, a mother, an avid reader, an occasional artist and potter, an erstwhile piano player and quilter, and the chief of staff to the family cat. Jan's life verse is John 3:16.

Find out more about Jan Thompson:
JanThompson.com

Subscribe to Jan's book news mailing list:
JanThompson.com/newsletter

For God so loved the world
that He gave His only begotten Son,
that whoever believes in Him
should not perish but have everlasting life.
—John 3:16